A TALENT FOR TROUBLE

A TALENT FOR TROUBLE

NATASHA FARRANT

CLARION BOOKS
Houghton Mifflin Harcourt
Boston New York

Perhaps I'm mad . . . but I think children must lead
big lives . . . if it is in them to do so.

Eva Ibbotson, *Journey to the River Sea*

Clarion Books
3 Park Avenue, New York, New York 10016

Copyright © 2018 by Natasha Farrant
First U.S. edition, 2019
First published in 2018 as *Children of Castle Rock* by Faber & Faber Limited,
Bloomsbury House, 74–77 Great Russell Street, London WC1B 3DA

Clarion Books is an imprint of
Houghton Mifflin Harcourt Publishing Company.

hmhbooks.com

The text was set in Adobe Garamond Pro.

Library of Congress Cataloging-in-Publication Data
Names: Farrant, Natasha, author.
Title: A talent for trouble / Natasha Farrant.
Description: First U.S. edition. | Boston ; New York : Clarion Books,
Houghton Mifflin Harcourt, 2019. | Summary: Originally published: London :
Faber & Faber Limited, 2018. | Summary: Eleven-year-old Alice Mistlethwaite persuades
her boarding school friends, Jesse and Fergus, to set out on an off-the-grid adventure
in which they face storms, illness, injury, and international jewel thieves.
Identifiers: LCCN 2019001086 (print) | LCCN 2019002590 (ebook)
ISBN 9781328580788 (hardback) | ISBN 9780358164364 (e-book)
Subjects: | CYAC: Adventure and adventurers—Fiction. | Boarding
schools—Fiction. | Schools—Fiction. | Friendship—Fiction. |
Survival—Fiction. | Scotland—Fiction. | BISAC: JUVENILE FICTION / Action
& Adventure / Survival Stories. | JUVENILE FICTION / Social Issues /
Friendship. | JUVENILE FICTION / Girls & Women. | JUVENILE FICTION /
Social Issues / Emotions & Feelings.
Classification: LCC PZ7.F2406 (ebook) | LCC PZ7.F2406 Tal 2019 (print)
DDC [Fic]—dc23 | LC record available at https://lccn.loc.gov/2019001086

Printed in the United States of America
DOC 10 9 8 7 6 5 4 3 2 1
4500775999

For Phoebe, most excellent of goddaughters, with thanks for her invaluable help.

A TALENT FOR TROUBLE

ONE

Goodbye, Cherry Grange

I MAGINE A HOUSE, in a garden. The paint is flaking and the chimney is cracked and the uncut grass is wild. But ignore all that. Look here instead, at the giant wisteria with a vine as thick as your arm, its purple flowers dripping against the old stone wall. Look at the swing hanging from that ancient oak, those cherry trees planted in a circle around the house. One of the trees is so close to a window that in summer, when it fruits, the girl who lives here can reach out to pick the cherries.

Imagine that—picking cherries from your bedroom window!

The house, Cherry Grange, was named for the trees. A man called Albert Mistlethwaite built it over a hundred years ago when he came home from a war, and his family has lived here ever since.

That's a lot of cherries, and pies, and cakes, and pots of jam.

We'll go inside now. Do you see those pale rectangles on the hall floor, those other pale rectangles on the walls? They were made by rugs and pictures, but those have gone now, along with all the furniture. There's nothing left but dust and sunlight.

Let's move on! Here is the kitchen—and here is the family, finishing breakfast.

Small, pale eleven-year-old Alice sits cross-legged on the counter with her nose in a book, tracing the words with her finger as she reads, chewing the end of one of her stiff dark braids. Her father, Barney (you may have seen him once on television), stands drinking coffee by the window with his back to the room, while his older sister, Alice's aunt Patience, in paint-spattered overalls, dries crockery at the sink.

The last of the Mistlethwaites, in their natural habitat. Take a good look—you'll not see this again. For the house is sold, and today they are moving out.

TWO

Shhh! Listen!

A BLOODCURDLING SCREECH BROKE the silence in the kitchen, followed by a series of thumps. Barney turned away from the window.

"The house," he observed, "is crying."

"It's just the wind in the chimney." Patience finished drying and began to stack crockery into a plastic crate. "It doesn't help being all dramatic. And hurry up with that mug."

A juddering moan—the water pipes—succeeded the thumps.

"*Revenge of Cherry Grange*," rasped Barney in a loud stage whisper. "That's what it would be called if it were a film. *The Curse of the Mistlethwaites. The Haunting of the Brown-Watsons.*"

The Brown-Watsons were the happy, bouncy family of six people and two Labradors who had bought Cherry Grange. All the Mistlethwaites loathed them, even Patience, who had actually wanted to sell the house.

"Barney, your mug!" she snapped now.

"All right, all right!" He drank the coffee and handed her the mug. "But just so you know, Alice has already written a story about the Brown-Watsons, and they all die except the dogs. It'd make a cracking film, wouldn't it, Alicat?"

Alice looked up from her book and blinked. "What?"

"We're talking about your story," said Barney. "And ghosts."

Patience shoved the crate at him. "Go and put this in the car," she said, then, "Alice, where are you going?"

Alice, at the mention of ghosts, had turned even paler and slid off the kitchen counter. Now, like scores of Mistlethwaites before her, she was opening the garden door with a practiced kick.

"Mum," she said.

"Your mum?" Patience looked baffled. "What are you talking about? Alice! Breakfast!"

But Alice was already gone.

It had rained in the night, and the grass was still wet. Uncut since the previous summer, in some places it reached almost to Alice's knees, soaking through her jeans. She didn't notice, and if she had noticed, she wouldn't have cared. She thumped through the grass and past the ring of cherry trees dropping the last of their blossoms, round the weed-choked pond where the heron came every spring to eat the tadpoles when they turned into frogs, past the butterfly bush and the lavender, until she arrived panting at the bench at the end of the garden.

She couldn't believe she had forgotten.

Her father and her aunt had yet to explain properly why they were leaving, but Alice was almost certain that if her mother hadn't died, none of this would be happening. Mum had loved Cherry Grange as if she had been born Clara Mistlethwaite instead of Clara Kaminska, and when she was alive, everything —everything!—had been better. The house had been full of noise, because Mum was always laughing and singing and dancing, and it had smelled delicious because she was an amazing cook, and they hadn't always been broke, because Mum had had a full-time job people actually paid her for, unlike Aunt Patience with her painting or poor Barney with his acting. But she was gone, killed by a fast and horrible illness four years earlier when Alice was seven, her ashes scattered in the garden and a white rosebush planted in her memory right where Alice was standing now, which was the exact spot where they had loved to sit together on summer evenings to read bedtime stories. Alice came here often to talk to her mother.

The bush was set against a wall, and it was strong and graceful, just like Mum had been, and covered in a riot of little pink buds which, when they opened, turned into big blowsy white roses. It was unthinkable never to see it flower again.

Alice picked up a stick and began to dig.

Patience, arriving on the scene a few minutes later, watched her with despair and wondered, yet again, if she had been wrong to sell the house.

Once a cheerful, outgoing girl, since her mother's death all Alice ever wanted was to stay at home to read and write. She wrote all the time, but most of all when Barney was away, filling the notebooks Patience bought her with stories she would present to him on his return. He was the only person who was allowed to read them. Alice worshipped her father, never questioning his long absences but clinging firmly to the belief that one day he would be a great actor. And they could have carried on like this forever—Alice scribbling away and not going out, and Barney traveling but not saying why, and Patience in the attic painting pictures nobody wanted to buy—except that Patience had snooped and read some of Alice's stories.

The stories were wild and sad and funny and beautiful. Until she read them, all Patience had wanted was to keep Alice safe and fed and well. After reading the stories, it became her secret wish to help Alice live as passionately as she wrote. And the more she thought about it, the clearer it became to her that what was needed was a complete break with the past. She was sure she was right—most of the time—almost sure—probably right. For weeks now, she had lain awake at night convincing herself . . . but when she saw her niece do things like try to dig up a rosebush with a stick, she did wonder if it was—well—kind, to take a young girl away from the only home she had ever known.

Alice never talked about her emotions—never talked much at all, in fact, her one-word exit from the kitchen being a typical example—but she couldn't hide them. Her eyes blazed with anger as Patience approached, even as she scrunched her nose to keep from crying.

"I'm not leaving without her," she said.

Patience sighed, knowing there would be no room in her small car for a rosebush. She looked around for Barney. Barney —as usual when there was something difficult to do—had disappeared. She would just have to tell Alice it wasn't possible.

A clean break, Patience thought.

Then, seeing the determined set of Alice's chin, *Sometimes you just have to make room.*

"There are still tools in the shed," she said. "I didn't see any point in getting rid of them. I'll get a spade, and we can dig it up properly. We'll have to cut it back, mind. Then we can put it in a pot."

"Her," Alice corrected, scrabbling away with her stick again. "Mum. We can put Mum in a pot."

It sounded funny, but neither of them laughed.

Goodbye! whispered the cherry trees. *Goodbye, goodbye,* from the sprawling attics with Patience's art studio and the den where Alice liked to write, from the banisters Mistlethwaite children always slid down and the green-tiled fireplace where they roasted chestnuts. Alice walked silently through every room, and heard the house's farewell in everything she touched.

It had nothing to do with pipes and chimneys.

They finished packing the car. It didn't take long, because they didn't have much—a few suitcases of clothes, a crate of crockery, some books, a silver teapot. Pictures, rugs, a vase.

A rosebush in a pot.

It wasn't a lot to show for over a hundred years.

They took one last look at the dear old house and squeezed into the car. For a wild, hopeful moment, Alice thought it wouldn't start, but then there was the familiar crunch of gravel beneath the tires, and they were driving through the wooden gates they would never drive through again, and they were in the lane, and there was the little bridge over the stream in which they had all paddled, and now they were turning onto the main road, and the house was gone, and there was a prick of blood on her arm where the rosebush had scratched her. She sucked the scratch to make the bleeding stop, and thought that if this were a story, she would make the rose or the car or even the blood into a portal to another world, one where cures were found to keep mothers alive and aunts did not inexplicably sell houses. But this wasn't a story, just people in a car, driving toward an unknown and terrifying future.

"To new adventures!" Barney cried, brandishing the silver teapot. "This is going to be fun!"

There would be no room for Barney in her story. There never was. Barney, for Alice, was above stories.

The Mistlethwaites don't see the Brown-Watsons' moving van when it passes, or the Brown-Watsons' people carrier that follows, and just as well. They don't want to know about Brown-Watson children tearing upstairs to fight over bedrooms, or Brown-Watson adults talking about which trees to fell, or Brown-Watson Labradors digging holes in the garden. And neither do we, frankly. Our story is with the Mistlethwaites, and we are going with them to London to put Alice on a train.

THREE

The End of the World

P OSSIBLY, WHEN YOU think of railway stations in major cities, you imagine high ceilings and giant clocks and everywhere the thrill of adventures about to begin. Jesse Okuyo—currently at London Euston Station, lugging his orange Stormy Loch Academy rucksack and his empty violin case after his three older brothers down the dark, poky platform of the Scottish sleeper train—would have loved such a station. Another lonely kid, at the age of just turned twelve, Jesse longed for adventure. One of his favorite things was to stride about the countryside with a map and a compass and binoculars, pretending to be a great explorer. Other favorite things included video games in which he got to destroy lots of monsters, books in which he could choose the ending, and stories about ancient heroes and medieval knights. Sometimes, when he read these, he substituted his name for theirs.

Jesse Okuyo slayed the dragon!

Jesse Okuyo charged into battle!

Reality was different.

Reality right now was distinctly unheroic, thanks to his brothers, who had all done this journey many times when they were students at Stormy Loch. Jared had stolen his violin and was skipping along ahead of him, playing a rowdy Scottish ballad. His brother Jed was dancing, and Jeremy was singing. People were staring. Some were taking photographs. They clearly thought this was very picturesque and charming. Maybe you do too. Jesse just wished his brothers were normal. And also not so good at singing, and dancing, and violin playing, or so good-looking, or so tall. Jesse was tall too, but next to them he felt like a hobbit.

His brothers had arrived at his car, were surrounding the smiling attendant, still playing and singing and dancing.

"What's the matter, little brother?" Jed crowed when Jesse caught up. "Don't you like our sendoff?"

"You know I don't," Jesse muttered as he pushed past them to climb aboard.

"WHAT?" cried Jed, leaping on after him.

"HE DOOOOESN'T LIKE OUR SENDOOOOFFFF!" sang Jeremy, bouncing on next.

Jared switched from the ballad to a tragic lament.

They waited until Jesse had struggled out of his rucksack, and then they pounced. Jeremy got him in a headlock. Jed began to tickle him. Jared moved on from the lament to a fast and furious jig. Jesse yelled, and swore, and tried to punch them. They didn't hear the commotion outside as the Mistlethwaites arrived, Aunt Patience in an apple-green coat waving Alice's ticket, Barney carrying an orange rucksack just like Jesse's, Alice herself clutching the battered copy of her favorite book, *Journey to the River Sea,* which she had read all the way in the car.

"Are we late?" cried Aunt Patience to the attendant (the Mistlethwaites were always late). "We got lost!" (The Mistlethwaites were always getting lost.)

The attendant informed them they had five minutes.

Onto the train the Mistlethwaites bundled, straight into the knot of laughing, fiddle-playing, roaring Okuyos blocking the narrow corridor outside Jesse's compartment.

"Let me go!" Jesse's voice was muffled, his face buried in Jeremy's belly.

"Not until you pee!" shouted Jed. "He pees when he's tickled," he informed the bewildered Mistlethwaites.

It was too much. With a final roar, Jesse threw off his captors and flung himself into his berth. For a few brief, appalled seconds before he slammed shut the door, he and Alice stared at each other.

"I think you two are going to the same school," murmured Aunt Patience.

Then *BANG!* went the door, and Jesse sank to the ground with his head on his knees.

Be careful what you wish for, they say.

Jesse wanted adventure. He had no idea that adventure had just found him.

Aunt Patience was sending Alice to boarding school.

Alice, horrified, had tried to resist. She had read hundreds of books about boarding school, she informed her aunt. Even the sunnier ones involved violent sports or people getting murdered or evil wizards luring innocents to the Dark Side.

Boarding schools, Alice had argued, were dangerous.

"They are nothing of the sort," Aunt Patience had responded (and oh, how she would one day regret saying that!). "Look, here's the website. It's a charming place. Like a storybook!"

"It'll be expensive," pleaded Alice, ignoring the website.

Aunt Patience said it wasn't as expensive as you might think, and added brightly that all the uniforms were handmade by the students, and that the school had its own farm where they grew their own food, because they believed in being self-sufficient and in what Aunt Patience called a Well-Rounded Education.

"Plus, it's in a castle," she said. "Called Stormy Loch. In Scotland!"

"Scotland!"

"It's not the end of the world."

"It's the end of the country. Where are *you* going to live?"

"I've told you before, darling. I've got a teaching job in London."

"But you hate cities. You're mad. This whole thing is mad."

At which point Aunt Patience had pursed her lips and clicked shut her laptop and pronounced those impossible grown-up words, "Well, I think it will be good for you."

Nor had Barney been any help.

"Sorry, Alicat," he said, when she burst into his room to beg him to change Aunt Patience's mind. "You know she never listens to me. Besides," he added as she threw herself into his arms, "Scotland's not so bad. And I'll come and visit, I promise! Here, look . . ." He reached into his pocket for his phone and tapped something into Google. "There was this place, I remember, an island—what was it called? Nish! That's the one—it was awesome. There were puffins, and a castle with a moat. I used to pretend I was the king." He waved his phone like an imaginary sword. "Pow! Zap! Take that, vile intruder!"

He held out his phone. Alice looked, and saw a photograph of thousands of gulls flying above a stormy sea.

The Isle of Nish is a paradise for ornithologists and seabirds, she read.

"An ornithologist is someone who studies birds," Barney said. "Isn't that great? I'll take you there! We'll be king and queen together!"

"I know what an ornithologist is," Alice said. "I want to live with you."

But Barney, it turned out, was going traveling. On tour, he said, and she pretended to believe him. She had not protested again, but brooded on her fears alone.

Now, standing on the train at Euston that was going to carry her through the night to the place of horrors where she would have to wield hockey sticks and be forever surrounded by people, rather than the safe familiar solitude of Cherry Grange, and probably sleep in a dorm with dozens of other girls who would force-feed her midnight feasts when she wanted to write, and possibly be petrified by a wizard — she couldn't believe it was happening. She buried her face in Barney's chest, inhaling the familiar smell of him, the smoky caramel of his leather jacket, the spiced lemon of his aftershave.

"When will you come?" she asked in a tiny voice.

A whistle blew before he could answer. He leaped off the train after Patience, then reached up his hand. Alice leaned out of the open window to take it, but already the train was pulling away, and he was running alongside it, shouting something she couldn't hear.

The train rounded a bend and, just like that, he was gone.

Alice pulled her head back inside and very carefully closed the window against the hot metallic air.

Soon. That was what she had heard. She was sure of it.

Soon, soon, soon . . .

Be careful what you wish for.

FOUR

Fluffy and Soft and Covered
in Penguins and Unicorns

THE TRAIN TRUNDLED through stations, past suburban houses and sharp-angled office buildings. Alice and Jesse saw nothing.

Alice sat on her bunk with her back to the window, furiously writing a marvelous story about a girl who ran away to join a circus and fly about on the high trapeze over a pit of starving tigers, while in the berth next door, Jesse lay on his back, staring at the ceiling and hating his brothers.

Adventures start in all sorts of ways. Jesse knew that in his place his brothers would not have felt humiliated. They would have laughed at Alice's horrified face and boasted about how much they peed. But Jesse, unlike them, was shy, and sensitive, and easily embarrassed. He worried about what other people thought of him. He imagined Alice right now lying on her own bunk, laughing at him.

If she was not to laugh at him forever, he would have to be brave, and explain.

He swung himself off the bunk, bowed (it helped to pretend he was entering a jousting tournament), stepped out into the corridor, and knocked on her door.

Each thought the other terrifying.

Alice, who hated to be interrupted when she was writing, opened the door with a black scowl that struck dread in Jesse's heart. And even though Jesse was the gentlest of souls, his mere presence—a real boarding-school boy!—was petrifying for Alice. He wasn't to know that strangers always rendered her mute. Faced with her silent stare, he was convinced that she despised him. And she could not guess that the choking sounds he made were meant to be friendly. She heard only growling, like the tigers in her story.

If it hadn't been for Jesse's brain wave, the whole thing would have been a disaster.

With a sort of yelp, he dived back into his berth. Then, with renewed courage, he returned, bearing a thermos and a large Tupperware box.

"Picnic," he said firmly, and squeezed past Alice into her berth.

And so it began, quietly, with tea and cake and sandwiches.

Cross-legged on Alice's bunk, they ate and drank together

in cautious silence until Jesse (still too crushed to mention his brothers) asked politely what brought her to Stormy Loch halfway through the year. Just as politely, she said that it was her aunt's idea. *She is banishing me* was what she really wanted to say. *Like the queen in Snow White. Or the stepmother in Hansel and Gretel. She's basically a witch.*

But these were far too many words.

"What is school like?" she forced out instead.

Sometimes, the simplest questions are the most difficult to answer, especially if you want to be truthful. Jesse, who like Alice wasn't much of a talker, pondered his reply. He could see that *OK, actually* or *Fine, if you like that sort of thing* would be unsatisfactory, but there was a lot to say about Stormy Loch, and he really had no idea where to begin. Instead, he produced an old smartphone of Jared's and pulled up the school website. On the screen, a group of teenagers and a strapping helmet-haired woman, all dressed in workmen's overalls, stood flourishing paintbrushes in front of a low stone building, each stone of which was painted a different color. The caption beneath read *Exploding Butterfly.*

Alice stared, baffled.

"They're Art Talents," Jesse explained. "That's the art teacher, Frau Kirschner. She's experimental."

"Art Talents?"

"Everyone has a talent. That's what the major says. Major

Fortescue," he clarified, "founded the school. He's all about helping people find their talent. Tap on another photograph."

The next picture was of a messy-haired redheaded boy with
sticking-out ears and train-track braces, holding up a silver cup
and grinning so widely Alice couldn't help grinning back. Jesse's
expression darkened.

"Fergus Mackenzie. Talent: Schoolwork." He spoke with
all the feeling of a person for whom schoolwork is not a talent
but a burden. Of all the people to be on the school website, no
one could have annoyed him more than Fergus. "Showing off
because he won the stupid Math Challenge. He's always showing
off."

Alice, who could have been good at schoolwork but whose
daydreaming drove her teachers mad, asked sympathetically
what Jesse's talent was.

"Running," Jesse mumbled gloomily, because being able to
run faster than anyone in your year when you had the longest
legs didn't feel like much of a talent at all, especially when your
brothers, when they were at school, forever came first in everything. Then he brightened, remembering. "But it's the Great
Orienteering Challenge this term — that's something else about
school, they love Challenges — and I'm really good at that. It's
like a massive orienteering competition for the whole year, and
I'm pretty sure I can win."

Alice (who had only a vague understanding of what orienteering was) said kindly that she was sure he could win too. Jesse, considerably cheered, asked what she was talented at.

"Writing, I suppose," she said. "Stories. Not schoolwork."

"That's amazing!" said Jesse (who had never written a story in his life). Then — because this was what he had come for, and she seemed nice, and if he didn't say it now he never would — "About earlier," he gabbled. "What my brother said. You know, the peeing thing. It was only once, and I was five years old, and already bursting. I promise I don't do it all the time."

And because he had shared his picnic with her, and told her she was amazing, she didn't laugh but replied very seriously, "Once, when I was little, Dad tickled me so hard I had to change my pants."

They had a long way to go before they could really call themselves friends. There would be at least two betrayals, and a few lies, and a couple of near-death experiences. But they didn't know that yet. They just knew they felt a whole lot better than they had when the journey started.

When Jesse had gone, Alice undressed and changed into her pajamas, which were too short at the ankles and wrists, but which she loved because they were fluffy and soft and covered in penguins and unicorns. It felt cozy to be tucked up in her narrow bunk, with the little light just above her pillow, safe from the dark world outside. And school seemed like maybe it would be all right, if other students were like Jesse. As she pulled down her window blind, she blew a kiss at the night sky, the way she always did when she was not with Barney. Then she picked up her notebook and carried on with her story, in which the girl in the circus made friends with a boy and freed the hungry tigers. She wrote and wrote and wrote, until she fell asleep with her head on the page.

The train sped on through the night. They stopped in Crewe, then Preston and Edinburgh, but Alice did not wake until the attendant knocked on her door the following morning. She opened her blind and caught her breath. At some point in the night, the long train had become three cars and was now traveling on a single-track line. The glass and concrete of Euston, the row houses and office buildings, had given way to mountains and heather and bracken. Alice saw a pool of water reflecting the sky, a circling bird of prey.

Deep inside her, something long forgotten began to stir.

It was like entering a different world.

They had arrived in Scotland.

FIVE

They Are All Mad

A SCHOOL BUS WAS supposed to meet them at Castlehaig, but when they got off the train, it wasn't there. As she climbed down from the train, Alice had felt cautiously optimistic. Now, standing on the deserted platform, all her fear and uncertainty returned, and if you ever pass through Castlehaig yourself, you will understand why. It is not, in the way most people understand it, a real station at all—just a grassy bit of platform with a broken bench in the middle of nowhere, with nothing but mountains all around and an unconvincing road.

"Late," said Jesse bitterly. "Again. It's always late, and it's not fair." Alice looked at him curiously, and he realized with a start that she didn't know about the First Day Challenge.

Which put Jesse in a dilemma.

The First Day Challenge was simple: the last person to arrive at school lost. If Alice had known about it, she would have understood why the bus being late wasn't fair. Jesse and Alice were the only two students who had taken the train. It was already past nine o'clock. School was a two-hour drive away, and the competition was getting fiercer every year, with people arriving earlier and earlier. Jesse should know—he had lost twice now, at the start of each of his two terms at Stormy Loch. It was becoming a family joke. And if there was one thing Jesse hated, it was being a joke.

If the bus didn't arrive soon, he and Alice would be last, and would be competing against each other.

It was only fair that she know.

He should easily beat Alice, because he was fast and she was small. But small people could be fast too. Unlike him, Alice was wearing full school uniform, whereas he was dressed for running. With her heavy jumper and blazer and school shoes, she would be at a distinct disadvantage.

Then again . . .

It was very tempting not to tell her.

But also unsporting, especially for sort-of friends. And being shy and not very talkative and overly worried about what people thought of him, Jesse was somewhat short of friends.

"I'm going to look out for the bus," he said, and scrambled up the side of a high crag to survey the road with his binoculars.

Alice's head swam and her stomach lurched as she watched him. Years ago, she would have been climbing right up there with Jesse. A little mountain goat, her mother used to call her, because she climbed everything. But since Mum died, Alice had been terrified of heights and couldn't climb a thing. Feeling very small, because of the mountains, and cold, because the uniform's lumpy orange sweater (hand-knitted by a former student and bought secondhand online) wasn't very warm, and slightly wobbly because of Jesse's climbing, she hugged her knees and watched the empty road and wondered what they should do if the bus didn't come.

"Could we walk?" she asked.

Once, when she was little, Barney had forgotten to pick her up from school. Alice had waited and waited while her teacher tried to call him, then walked the two miles home on her own. Her father had laughed his big warm laugh when he found out, and called Alice a little trouper. Patience had been furious, but Alice had loved how proud he was of her.

"Walking would take days." Jesse sighed.

"Phone?"

"No signal."

"What, none at all?" She thought with panic of Barney. "What about at school?"

"None there either."

"But how do you keep in touch?"

"You write. You know, letters."

"Letters?" She wasn't sure Barney had ever written a letter. He was more a talking kind of person.

"Or you can send emails from the library."

"The library?"

But a small red dot had appeared on the distant horizon, and Jesse was half sliding, half scrambling down from the crag.

"Run!" he yelled, picking up both their rucksacks and throwing her his violin case.

"What?" She squinted toward the road. "But it's miles away!"

"RUN!"

Alice ran.

The minibus slowed down just enough for them to climb in before taking off again with a screech of tires, flinging Alice to the floor.

"Whoops!" The driver, a twelfth-year girl called Tatiana with a Talent for Mechanics, slammed on the brakes just long enough for Alice to stagger into a seat. "Seat belts on!"

They swung into a U-turn, then sped back in the direction the bus had come. Jesse felt a surge of optimism that maybe they wouldn't be last after all, and he wouldn't have to beat Alice.

"How are your lovely brothers, little Okuyo?" asked Tatiana.

Jesse's optimism evaporated. Anxiety returned.

"Just get us there as fast as you can," he mumbled.

The bus flew over a humpbacked bridge as Tatiana, laughing, leaned forward to turn on the radio. A crackling pop song came on. Tatiana sang along, dancing in her seat. Silently, Alice braced her feet and gripped her armrest and thought, *They are all mad.*

". . . a unique jade figurine has been stolen from a private home in Rome," announced the radio, suddenly clear as they crested another hill. "A . . . *(crackle)* . . . million-euro reward is . . . *(crackle) (crackle)* . . . information . . ."

"Imagine having a million euros!" cried Tatiana, hurtling round a bend. "I'd buy a sports car. A Maserati!"

"I'd buy a helicopter," grumbled Jesse.

"The carving depicts a boy riding a dragon and is about the size of a plum."

"Plum, tiddly plum!" sang Tatiana, swerving to avoid a sheep, and Alice tried very hard to think of her circus story, where she found her heroine had been kidnapped by the tiger tamer, who was driving about like a lunatic in search of his missing cats.

On they drove, on and on. They entered a narrow valley. The sky darkened and hailstones the size of Ping-Pong balls pelted the minibus.

"Stupid Scottish weather," said Tatiana, slowing down.

"Can we really not go faster?" asked Jesse.

"Do you really want to die?" Tatiana replied, while in Alice's story the tiger tamer plowed into a snowdrift and the circus girl gave up and burst into tears.

The hail stopped as suddenly as it had started. They turned off the road into a layby fringed with dark pines and dotted with flooded potholes, with a pretty hand-decorated sign saying SROMTY LOCHE KAR PARC.

"Painted by Agnes Bartleby in Year Nine," said Tatiana. "Talent for Crafts. Not spelling."

This was where Stormy Loch students were dropped off, to be taken the rest of the way in minibuses, because the road beyond was too narrow for lots of cars going up and down.

The car park was empty.

Which meant they were last.

Jesse's heart, already low, sank further. He was going to have to beat Alice.

Slowly now, creakily, the bus began to climb, through woods and past waterfalls, until it entered a bleak, bare valley with slopes of smashed scree and short, pale grass. The road here was straight and flat. Tatiana whooped and floored the accelerator, narrowing her eyes as the bus hurtled toward a rock face. Alice almost cried with relief after they roared through a narrow pass.

They slammed to a halt. Jesse undid his seat belt and prepared to run.

Alice, speaking for the first time, croaked, "Are we there?"

"Not exactly," said Tatiana.

Ahead of the minibus, the road dropped in hairpin bends through woods of fir and pine toward a lush, perfectly contained valley, its floor a patchwork of stone-walled fields dotted with cows and sheep and goats. To the west lay the lake itself, Stormy Loch, a silver sheet in which the surrounding mountains were reflected like a perfect upside-down world. To the east stood the castle, built of pale gray stone, with a pointed turret in each corner and twelve tall windows standing six each side like guards posted at its arched front door. An ancient tower, the original keep, stood in a copse beyond the castle, ivy twisting round its crumbling walls and rooks swirling about its roof, its dark brown bricks smothered with yellow lichen. It leaned perilously to one side.

Patience had been right — it was like a storybook, and a sinister one, at that.

"Right, out you get!" said Tatiana, and the first betrayal was set in motion as Jesse scrambled for the door.

SIX

Race!

THE NEXT FEW seconds were a blur. Jesse ran. Alice, clueless, did not. Tatiana, seeing her bewilderment, bellowed, "OKU-YO! COME BACK HERE!"

Jesse slunk back to the bus.

"You didn't tell her, did you?" Tatiana accused him. "She doesn't know."

"Tell . . . tell me what?" faltered Alice.

"From here on in," said Tatiana, "it's a race. It's a rule. The last person to touch the front door loses. Honestly, Jesse! That whole journey up from London and you never thought to tell her?"

Jesse looked at the ground.

"Oh, I get it!" Tatiana laughed unpleasantly. "You did think of telling her, but you wanted to be sure to win! Jesse, she's half your size! Did you really think she'd beat you?"

Jesse mumbled something about small people being better

at long distances, and to look at professional athletes and the Olympics. Tatiana said something rude about professional athletes.

"But why?" asked Alice.

"Never you mind," said Tatiana grandly. "I'm canceling the race."

Jesse was outraged. "You can't do that!"

"I can, and I will! I'm considerably older than you, Jesse Okuyo, which means I get to do exactly what I want. And what I want is for you two to walk nicely together right up to the front door, and share the Consequence. I'm so sorry" — she turned to Alice — "I can't do better than that. Literally nobody takes the train anymore, not since school forgot to pick up a bunch of kids and they had to spend the night at Castlehaig. That was before I was driving, of course. I've never forgotten anybody. Well, *do svidaniya*, as we say in Russia! Toodle-pip!"

And with a toot of the horn, she left.

Alice and Jesse walked together along the winding road, and it was as though something had broken.

"I wanted to tell you," Jesse said. "I just couldn't find the right moment."

Alice could have pointed out that there had been plenty of right moments over the past fourteen hours for Jesse to speak, but she didn't. Instead, she thought about her story, when her circus girl made friends with a boy and freed the tigers. Writing that bit had felt lovely. Now it turned out that the boy wasn't really a friend after all.

It was confusing.

Perhaps, if she had spoken, Jesse would not have done what he did. As it was, walking beside her in uncomfortable silence, he began to grow indignant. It wasn't his fault, after all, if Alice didn't know about the First Day Challenge. All the details were there on the school website. And as the fresh mortification of Tatiana's onslaught subsided, he told himself that there were rules for this Challenge, and she couldn't just go around breaking them, flinging her weight about because she was nearly eighteen and the major let her drive. Jesse himself never broke rules. He was famous for it, so famous that Fergus Mackenzie (who broke rules all the time) would salute when he passed him and call him Captain Fussypants.

The point of the First Day Challenge was that there was only one rule: the last person to touch the front door LOST.

And Jesse didn't want to lose.

His feet itched. His legs tingled. Every bit of his body wanted to run.

They reached the valley floor, and the road was straight now, flanked on either side by pink and purple rhododendrons. Ahead was a pair of rusty gates, set in mossy pillars on which sat two chipped stone griffins. Alice's apprehension grew.

Suddenly, she wanted her mother.

"This is it," said Jesse in a strangled voice. "School."

Beyond the gates, the road curved through more rhododendrons and disappeared. He tried to picture the scene at school right now. Usually, on the first day back, the courtyard was full of students, cheering on the racers as they arrived from the minibuses. Even on the two occasions when he had arrived last and alone, running for all he was worth to prove that even though he had lost he wasn't a loser, they had been there. Would they be cheering now? Or would they have disbanded, as disgusted as he was that Tatiana had canceled the race?

Would the major accept Tatiana's decision?

He wanted so badly to run.

Alice, pale to start with, had grown paler. Jesse could see she was nervous. He cast back to his own first day—he had been mortified at this point, knowing he had lost, but he had been excited too. Stormy Loch, at last! His brothers' school! But then, he had been here many times already on Visitors' Days. He wondered how it must feel to arrive knowing nothing.

Very difficult, he told himself firmly as his feet twitched.

He felt sorry for her, he convinced himself as his legs prickled.

And then—ah, and then Jesse could take it no more! He

didn't care what Tatiana had ordered. He couldn't just walk up to school, couldn't ignore tradition, couldn't face the humiliation, yet again, of being last.

Sometimes it just feels impossible to do what is right.

If Jesse could have seen himself running, perhaps he wouldn't have been so scornful of his talent. He ran like a champion on his long, strong legs, and it was plain to anyone looking that he loved it. Jesse running was a beautiful sight — a miracle of movement.

Alice, in contrast . . . Alice did not run like a long-distance Olympic athlete. Really, when she took off after him, she looked more like a small and furious terrier, and she trailed behind. The road sloped upward after the bend. She ran through the pain of her ragged breath, panted over the top of the hill . . . and there it was. Stormy Loch, the school itself, and in its gravel courtyard scores of students, ignoring Tatiana, were cheering them on, and they were terrifying . . .

And then — oh, Jesse . . .

Never look back when you're running. At best, it slows you down. At worst . . . at worst . . .

Jesse stumbled and fell. Alice's feet, despite her heavy school shoes, grew wings. She sailed past him, resisting the urge to kick him. The cheers from the crowd grew deafening. She could see the door, the lion's-head knocker gleaming, and Jesse was still behind her . . . For one glorious, triumphant moment she was sure she was going to win!

And then—

And then Fergus Mackenzie, the boy with the grin who drove Jesse mad, the red-haired genius and breaker of rules, stuck his foot right in her path.

As Jesse Okuyo flew past her, finally breaking his losing streak, Alice fell face first into a puddle.

SEVEN

The Major

FROM HIS STUDY at the top of the southwestern turret, Major Fortescue watched.

The room was a long way up, especially for a man with a cane, and it was impractical, being completely round and unsuited to almost all furniture, but it was worth it for the view. Up here, with the help of his old service binoculars, the major's one good eye could see everything.

This is what he saw, on that April morning.

He saw a rowdy group of Year Eights at the end of the loch, trying to push each other out of boats. He saw Agnes Bartleby, she of sign-painting fame, spray-paint a giant flower mural on top of the Exploding Butterfly. Around eleven, he saw Tatiana maneuver the bus with unconvincing caution into its hangar, and some little time later he saw Alice and Jesse, running, and Fergus sticking out his foot.

"Hmm," said the major, thoughtfully stroking his beard.

Patience Mistlethwaite had been to visit during the holidays, in secret, to meet him and to assess the school for Alice.

"My niece is stuck in the past," she had told him, before adding mysteriously, "She needs a new story—not to write, to live."

There were plenty of stories to be had, here in the valley in the mountains by the loch. The question was, mused the major, which one was right for Alice?

From a crate by the fire came a feeble mew. He stumped over to it and struggled to his knees. Nestled in an old fleece blanket were six very young kittens, rescued by the major during the holidays from Morag, who ran the school farm and had been going to drown them. He held out his hand, and the smallest kitten crawled into his palm. Too many waifs and strays, his grandmother always used to say when he brought home broken animals—a cat hit by a car, a fox caught in a trap, most thrillingly a shrew dropped from the sky by an eagle. He had been collecting lost souls ever since.

The kitten purred, kneading the major's hand with tiny paws. The major chuckled. Then, casting his eye to the courtyard below, he saw that a revolution was taking place. He put the kitten in the pocket of his alarmingly green jacket, made for him by a long-departed boy with a Talent for Fashion, and instantly forgot about it.

Fergus, Jesse, and Alice, he mused as he limped heavily down the ancient spiral staircase. An unlikely story, but why not?

Why ever not, indeed.

Madoc Jones had never intended to become a geography teacher. Until a few months before our story, he had worked for an international wildlife charity and had been engaged to be married. But then his fiancée had run away to Costa Rica, and shortly after that he had lost his job and had gone fishing in Scotland to think about love and life and the future, and had met the major, who had offered him a job.

"I can't guarantee it will mend your heart," the major had said. "But my school is in a beautiful place, and that will make you feel better."

Madoc knew only a little more about geography than the students, but he had turned out to be a fine teacher. He liked his subject and his pupils. He loved living in the valley. He just felt, sometimes, a little challenged by the school's rules.

"The person who knocks last on the front door is on wake-up duty for the rest of term," he informed a mud-sopped Alice, shouting to make himself heard over the clamor of students offering their views on the race. "He or she does this by beating the giant gong in the entrance hall three times, just as the clock strikes seven. The person who arrives last, in effect, becomes the person who rises first. It's called reveille, which is a military term referring to a bugle or trumpet call to wake up troops . . ."

Alice glared silently. She knew what *reveille* meant.

"You don't have to do it on Saturdays and Sundays," Madoc offered weakly.

"There wasn't meant to be a race." Tatiana bustled forward, pushing everyone else aside. "I abolished it."

The idea of students abolishing rules was a completely new one to Madoc. "Can you do that?" he asked.

Tatiana shrugged, like she didn't really care.

"The girl would have won if it hadn't been for Fergus," someone shouted. "He tripped her."

"No, I didn't!" Fergus lied.

Someone else produced a phone with a supposed video of the race, and passed it through the crowd to Madoc. The video was mainly of people's heads.

"Make Fergus do reveille!" someone shouted.

"No, make Jesse do it!" someone else shouted back. "It wasn't a proper win!"

"The whole system is barbaric!" Attention was momentarily diverted by the spectacular appearance of Frau Kirschner, the art teacher, wearing nothing but a black bathing suit and generous dabs of bright blue clay. "I do not believe in these Challenges.

They are anti-democratic. Every child should be free, like a beautiful bird. Also, the school should buy alarm clocks."

"I agree with you in principle," mused Professor Voroyev, the philosophy teacher. "But can you replace an entire belief system with alarm clocks?"

"What do you say, Jesse?" Madoc asked.

Jesse, who was not enjoying his victory, mumbled that he didn't know.

"But did you agree not to run?"

"There are rules," he argued, and instantly regretted it when half his year group groaned.

"Shame!" someone shouted.

"BARBARIC!" thundered Frau Kirschner.

"Fergus should do it!" shouted the crowd.

"No, Jesse!"

"Fergus! Jesse! Fergus! Jesse!"

"QUIET!"

The crowd fell silent. The major had arrived.

Even in his bright green jacket with a kitten wriggling in his pocket, the major could not fail to impress. There were the active reminders of his years in the Forces—the patch over his left eye blinded in the Balkans, the limp from a bad break in Afghanistan. But there was also the hard glitter of his good eye, the massive shoulders, the wild beard he never quite had the patience to trim. He regarded Alice in silence. She raised her chin and tried to return his gaze but found it just wasn't possible.

"Miss Mistlethwaite." It was a gentle foghorn of a voice, low and booming. "I'm afraid you will not like what I am going to say."

Alice's eyes widened.

"Someone must sound reveille, Miss Mistlethwaite," he said. "Just as someone must sound the gong for breakfast and lunch and tea and dinner, and the end of classes and the beginning of study hall. The race is simply a way of determining who. It is not a punishment. We do not have punishments at Stormy Loch; we have Consequences. All actions have Consequences, and we must accept them. It is how we make our rules, and are able to live as a well-ordered community. Do you understand?"

Alice did not understand but nodded anyway. The major turned his attention to Fergus.

"And, Mr. Mackenzie. Since you seem so entertained by muddy puddles, you will help clean the pigpen for the rest of term."

There were pigs? Faced with a whole new source of bewilderment, Alice felt exhausted.

"Do you agree that cleaning the pigpen is a suitable Consequence for your actions, Mr. Mackenzie?"

"Yes, sir," Fergus muttered.

"Then our work here is finished." The major beamed. "Welcome to Stormy Loch, Miss Mistlethwaite! Mr. Okuyo, Mr. Mackenzie, I am putting you in charge of our new student. Look after her well, show her around the school. Good grief, what on earth is that?"

The kitten, bored with the major's pocket, was climbing up his sleeve. Half a dozen Year Seven girls instantly surged around the headmaster. Alice, Fergus, and Jesse were forgotten.

Alice stared at the kitten.

"He rescues things," Jesse murmured. "Last term it was a baby rook; this term it's kittens. Look, Alice, I'm really sorry, truly I am. I just couldn't stop . . ."

He trailed off as Alice narrowed her eyes.

Fergus ran his hands through his hair and said, "Pigs!" Both the others eyed him with dislike.

"It serves you right," Jesse said. "What were you thinking, tripping her up?"

"Oh, shut up, Fussypants." Fergus, who was already feeling like an idiot for what he'd done—pigs!—felt that he did not need a lecture. "I helped you win."

"I don't need anybody's help!" Jesse snarled.

Alice sighed loudly and marched toward the front door. The boys stared, then ran after her.

EIGHT

I Know What a Pyromaniac Is

EVEN THE MOST rebellious Stormy Lockers (yes, that is what they call themselves) feel a thrill of pride on showing off the entrance hall. True: rather like Cherry Grange, it has seen better days. Two panes of the twelve tall windows are still boarded up after that ill-advised indoor cricket match last summer. The stag heads hanging gloomily on the wall are almost bald; those suits of armor flanking the foot of the staircase are more rust than metal. And don't get me started on the dust—all the housework at Stormy Loch is done by Lockers themselves, and they're just not very interested. But Lockers do love those suits of armor, which go by the names of Lord Alastair and Lord Hamish, and every night when they go up to bed, they pat the stags (which may account for the baldness).

As for the rest—look at the sweeping staircase, like something out of a film! The ceiling decorated with coats of arms!

The vast stone fireplace with its leering gargoyles! You could fit a whole class in that fireplace, if you stuffed a few of the smaller students up the chimney. So, gloomy, a little. Not very clean, I grant you. But awesomely impressive?

Yes! Yes! Yes!

Alice—wet, humiliated, confused—tried not to let these splendors cow her. The boys led her in and, as everyone always did for new visitors, stopped reverently just inside the front door, expecting the usual gasps of admiration. Alice kept her small nose stuck in the air and said nothing.

"Well, here's the gong," said Jesse awkwardly. He led her to an alcove to the left of the fireplace, where a giant brass disc stood suspended in an oak frame almost as tall as Alice. A mallet with a brown leather head the size of a tennis ball hung from a hook beside it.

"Reveille's OK, really," he said. "It'll be better this term, because it's light in the mornings. Last term it was dark, and freezing, especially when the boiler broke down . . ."

Alice folded her arms and stared at the ceiling. Jesse, not noticing the wobble of her lower lip, wished that it were yesterday again, and that they were back on the train and she was asking him about school. "There's this race," he would say, and today they would have run it fair and square, and he would almost certainly have won it, but properly, and now they would still be friends.

Timidly, he picked up the mallet and held it out to her.

"You hit the gong three times, as close to the middle as you can," he explained. "Do you want to try?"

Alice passed him without a word.

Sometimes you can wish all you like, but it won't change anything. Jesse, silenced, followed her meekly up the stairs.

The first-floor landing had a bare wooden floor and scuffed walls, one painted red, the other blue.

"Cost saving!" Fergus, who (as Jesse had said on the train) did like to show off, but also wanted to make amends for his idiotic behavior, took up the role of tour guide. "The major gets people to donate paint. He says it doesn't matter what color. He thinks it's cheerful. Observe the brightness of the red! Behold the soothing nature of the blue!"

Alice scowled. Fergus tried not to feel discouraged.

On they went, down a pink and yellow corridor—So light! So pretty! So like icing on a cake!—up one narrower flight of stairs and then another as Fergus rattled off information, pointing out classrooms and labs, common rooms and dorms, until finally they reached the top floor, and a lilac corridor with a lot of green doors.

They stopped in front of the last door.

"And this," announced Fergus with a bow and a flourish, "is your room."

Homesickness slammed into Alice the moment she walked in.

Until now, it had felt almost like a story happening to someone else. The train, the mad drive, the insane race . . . But the quiet little room she now found herself in felt real.

It wasn't unpleasant. The walls were painted the same soft lilac as the corridor; the bed was narrow but covered in a thick, squishy duvet; the view outside her small casement window was impressive. It was just those words—*your room.*

Your room belonged to a completely different place.

Alice puckered her brow as tears threatened to well up.

"You're very lucky," Jesse hazarded. "Most Year Sevens sleep in dorms, but this room just happened to be free. The girl who had it before you was in Year Twelve."

"She was expelled because she kept setting the chemistry lab on fire," said Fergus, looking up. "I guess she tried to burn this too."

Alice followed his gaze to a large black patch on the ceiling.

"She was helping Professor Lawrence with her fireworks," he continued. "Professor Lawrence is the chemistry teacher, and she's inventing a new kind of daytime firework for Visitors' Day, to set off from the middle of the loch. The major said Melanie

—Melanie van Boek, she was the girl who lived here before—had a Talent for Science, but honestly, she was one hundred percent a pyromaniac—that's a person who burns things down on purpose, in case you didn't—"

"I know what a pyromaniac is," said Alice, finally breaking her silence.

"Do you?" Fergus was delighted. "I'm collecting maniacs. There's pyromaniac, of course, to do with fire. And kleptomaniac, which is a person who can't stop stealing. And ablutomaniac, which is when you can't stop . . ."

"Washing." Alice sighed.

Fergus was impressed. "And bibliomaniac . . ."

"Books." Alice rolled her eyes, exasperated. "Obviously."

Jesse had no idea what they were talking about. He only knew that it was bad enough that Alice wasn't talking to him, without having her launch into incomprehensible conversations with Fergus. He tried to think of something clever to say—something that wasn't *Shut up, Fergus*—and couldn't.

"Dinomaniac!" cried Fergus.

Alice pushed him out of the room. Jesse hovered and tried to apologize again. She pushed him out too.

Fergus Mackenzie was the sort of smart that plays chess against computers, would rather do math puzzles than watch TV, and hacks into people's computers just because he can (remember that, it's important). He could read fluently in English by the age of four, in his mother's native German by five. By seven, he had taught himself Italian. By the age of ten, he had too many trophies for debating, math, and general brilliance to display.

Nobody disputed that he was a genius. Nobody even minded. What they did mind was that he played really, really stupid pranks. Like putting a toad in Esme's bed or salt in Amir's tea, or tying Joshua's bootlaces together before rugby practice. He wasn't even intelligently stupid. When Fergus was bored—and he was easily bored—he became positively imbecilic, and sometimes even mean. He had tripped Alice for literally no reason other than to see what would happen (and it had, he felt, been extremely satisfactory—all those people shouting at each other, and even the pigs were something new).

But as he and Jesse showed Alice around the school—the loch that changed color depending on the weather, the rowboats they used to go fishing, the farm where they grew their food, the spooky old keep that housed the new music rooms—he became fascinated by her. She had remained entirely silent all afternoon. At first he was disappointed, because he had enjoyed their brief exchange about manias and had hoped for more. But then—I told you he was smart—he became interested in her silence.

Alice's silence, Fergus felt, had the tightly wound quality of a kettle about to boil, or a baby about to scream, or a bomb about to explode. Which is to say that Alice's silence was very, very loud indeed.

At dinner, which she hardly touched, he watched as she answered the questions from the other Year Sevens who flocked to their table to meet her, nosy Jenny and shy Samira, little Duffy and Amir "the philosopher" and spotty Zeb. He saw that she was very still, and very poised, and very careful.

Not open, but not rude either — actually rather fascinatingly neutral, except for an interesting tic, her left hand moving as if she were writing. The only time she revealed anything interesting was when nosy Jenny asked what her father did.

"He's an actor," Alice said a bit too quickly.

"Is he famous?"

"Almost." And here Fergus, enthralled, saw that she actually blushed. "I mean, he will be. He's really good. He just needs a lucky break."

Fergus could guess what she was doing. He knew all about denial — he had been shocked the year before when his parents told him they were getting divorced, though looking back, all the signs had been there clear as day for him to see — the shouting and fighting, the constant traveling, the sleeping in separate rooms. *The eye sees what the heart desires,* the therapist his parents sent him to had said.

Whether she knew it or not, Alice Mistlethwaite was lying about her dad.

Fergus rather liked that.

NINE

A Talent for Trouble

F OR A HEARTBEAT, as she woke on her first morning, Alice thought she was still at Cherry Grange. Light filtered in around the curtains as it had at home, and the duvet had the same comforting snuggliness. She turned off the alarm and burrowed back down. She wasn't going anywhere until Patience called her for school . . .

School!

She opened her eyes again, and saw the sooty patch on the ceiling. The snuggly feeling gave way to dread. She looked at the time. It was six forty-five . . .

She groaned as she remembered, slid out of bed, and went over to the window. There was the loch—almost black today —and there were the mountains, the sky, and the wind-tossed clouds . . . She pulled off her pajamas and pulled on her lumpy uniform. Still yawning, she stepped into the lilac corridor. And now here were the green doors, and the narrow staircase, the pink and yellow landing like a cake, the cheerful red and blue one, and here was the entrance hall with its patched-up windowpanes . . .

The castle was eerily quiet in the early morning—the sort of quiet that plays tricks on the imagination. *What if they are watching me?* Alice wondered as she passed the glassy-eyed stag heads, and did someone speak as she passed the rusty suits of armor?

Here was the gong, and was there something lurking in the shadows of its recess? She picked up the mallet. It looked old. She wondered who had been the first person ever to use it.

The clock on the wall struck seven.

Alice hit the gong exactly as Jesse had instructed, right in the middle, and as the castle exploded with its boom and vibrations shot up her arm, she felt the thin line between reality and her imagination rip.

BOOM!

The stags were leaping from the wall . . . The suits of armor were creaking back to life . . .

BOOM! BOOM!

Somewhere on a three-mast ship on the open seas, a tiger roared, and a circus girl climbed the rigging with the wind in her hair. Alice swung the mallet again, harder, and it felt like all the stories she had ever written were flowing out of her, and as they swirled about her like living things, so did the emotions she had kept silent for so long — anger and sadness and fear — except they weren't silent anymore but turned into music by the mallet and the brass disc, making the air shake.

BOOM! Take that, Fergus Mackenzie, for tripping her up, and take that, Jesse Okuyo, for breaking his promise! As Alice smashed the reveille gong, she thought of every person who had ever made her furious. *BOOM! BOOM!* Take that, hateful Brown-Watsons, for stealing her house! Take that, Aunt Patience, for sending her away! *BOOM! BOOM!* The rage grew wilder. TAKE THAT, MUM, FOR DYING, AND BARNEY FOR . . .

"What do you think you are doing?"

The whirl of sound faded. The air stopped spinning and deposited Alice gently back on the ground, where she saw a small, stout woman dressed in a puce quilted bathrobe, her hair rolled into baby-blue curlers and her face purple with indignation.

Alice stared at her in astonishment.

"I am Matron," the small, stout woman announced, "and I am ordering you to give me that mallet! Three strikes! Did nobody explain? What you are doing now is the fire alarm! Just look at the commotion you've caused."

Slowly, Alice looked up. The entire student body were trooping down the stairs in their pajamas, some of them dragging their duvets.

Matron held out an imperious hand. "Young lady, relinquish that mallet!"

But Alice wasn't ready to relinquish anything.

Alice, who never showed her emotions.

Alice, who had been so quiet for so long.

BOOM! BOOM!! BOOM!!!

Take that, Matron, with your purple face and curlers and "young lady" and "commotion"!

"Upstairs, this minute!" shouted Matron, snatching away the mallet.

Up Alice went, cheeks flushed but head held high, a small smile tugging at the corners of her mouth, as the students watched in wonder.

Her aunt wanted her to live as she wrote. It looked as if Patience was going to get more than she'd bargained for.

The major, standing draped in kittens in the doorway of his study, wondered if dreamy Alice Mistlethwaite might be developing a Talent for Trouble.

TEN

Humongously, Enormously, and Superlatively Sorry

J ESSE HAD SPENT most of the night worrying. The more he thought about his behavior—he, the fastest runner in his year, taking off without warning to beat someone half his size—the less he liked himself. He cringed when he tried to see himself through his classmates' eyes.

No knight of old would have behaved as he had.

Worse, though, was that he liked Alice. He thought about the train again. He had liked the quiet, serious way they had spoken, the fact that she hadn't laughed at his explanation about his brothers, her own funny, generous admission. He had felt a connection with her. He couldn't believe he had thrown it away.

Shortly before dawn on that first day, he decided to make his peace with her by offering to share reveille, and resolved to get up early to show her the ropes. Immeasurably relieved, he fell asleep and only woke, like the rest of the castle, to the sound of Alice's explosive gonging.

And now he was confused, because he was sure he had explained what she was to do. It didn't occur to him that Alice might simply not care about how things were done—his brain didn't work like that. He decided to explain again at breakfast. But when he came into the dining hall, she was already sitting with Samira and Jenny.

He saw her ahead of him on her own as they filed into assembly. He quickened his pace to catch up with her—then shrank back, because Fergus had got there first.

"So I want you to know that I am humongously, enormously, and superlatively sorry for yesterday," Fergus said as he fell into step beside Alice. "Sometimes I behave like an idiot. Ask anybody! I'm famous for it. But I also want to say that what you did this morning with the gong was one hundred percent awesome."

Just because she had roused the whole school with a fake fire alarm did not make her suddenly talkative or trusting. She stared at him suspiciously.

"So awesome," insisted Fergus, before breaking into an excellent imitation of Matron. "Alice Mistlethwaite, look at the commotion you have caused! Surrender that mallet!"

Alice's lips twitched. Fergus beamed approvingly.

A few rows behind them, Jesse watched, and bristled.

Alice wasn't sure what she'd expected from assembly at Stormy Loch, but it certainly wasn't for it to be as dull and ordinary as at her old school. A succession of teachers stood up to talk about sports events and orchestra rehearsals. Morag Hamilton, the farmer, talked about what was growing in various polytunnels. Madoc talked about the Great Orienteering Challenge. Alice remembered how excited Jesse had been when he told her about this.

She glanced toward him and felt something tug at her heart when he looked away. She had liked him too, yesterday on the train. It might have all gone wrong since then, but she couldn't remember when she had liked anybody.

Sighing, she turned her attention back to the stage, where Matron was talking about the housework rotation.

"Not that anyone actually does the housework," whispered Fergus.

The major came on, and the assembly veered into the surreal as he asked for volunteers to help with his rescued kittens.

The major had a lot to say about kittens.

He talked about the difference between cow milk and kitten milk.

He lingered on the importance of regular feeding.

He paid particular attention to toilet training.

"After feeding, the mother cat would habitually lick the genitals and tummies of her babies to stimulate toileting," he boomed. "She would then clean them by eating their feces."

"What's feces?" whispered a girl called Esme, who was sitting on the other side of Alice.

"Poop," said Fergus.

"What? That's disgusting! No way am I volunteering for that!"

"No way!" echoed Esme's best friend, Zuzu.

Alice's laughter bubbled up suddenly, surprising her as much as the morning's gonging.

"It's true," whispered Fergus. "Feces are poop."

"I know what feces are," she whispered back.

And oh, the deliciousness of trying not to laugh! Alice's shoulders shook, and her face turned red, and her eyes began to stream, and the giggling was infectious because now Fergus was snorting, and leaning forward on his knees pressing the heels of his hands into his eyes, as if that could stop the gales of laughter building up from his stomach, and the laughter spread to Jenny, and Amir, and Samira until most of Year Seven were sniggering and snuffling, except Esme and Zuzu, who thought the others were too childish for words, and Jesse, who stared ahead eaten up with jealousy because Alice was laughing not with him, but with Fergus Mackenzie.

And so, with rituals and meals and alliances, a new term

began. Finally, they were liberated. The Year Sevens shuffled away to math, where Fergus was immediately set extra-difficult problems, Jesse agonized as numbers swum meaninglessly on the page, and Alice smiled politely and pretended to pay attention, but wrote out in her math book the bones of a new story, in which the kittens became miniature, magical tigers that performed rescue missions when called to action by the beating of a magical gong.

Three young people, all very different. All, in their own way, waifs and strays. All searching for something, though none of them knew quite what.

All unaware, as yet, that they might find it in one another.

ELEVEN

We'd Be Mad to Try It

DEAR DAD,

I've been here three weeks today! I know it seems incredible, but it's true.

Life at school continues better than expected. In French, Madame Gilbert, who is really a playwright, is making us be villagers in a market square. We have to say things like "Trois carottes, s'il vous plaît! Je suis un enfant, je ne comprends pas!" which means "Three carrots, please! I am a child, I don't understand!" So that will be useful one day (maybe), but for now she says we are not passionate enough about vegetables. In geography, we spend most of our time logging wildlife sightings for Mr. Madoc, because he is really a zoologist and not a geography teacher at all, and sad because his fiancée ran away to Costa Rica to rescue sea turtles and didn't want to marry him anymore. I don't know why. Yesterday in "class" (really a field at the end of the valley), I counted three hares, twelve rabbits, and a skylark, and he was very pleased and smiled and was actually almost good-looking. Oh, and in art, we all have to paint ourselves with blue mud called woad and pretend to be an ancient Scottish tribe called Picts, fighting off Romans. Our teacher, Frau Kirschner, says we are an Installation, and she is calling us "Democracy Failing." She says it's Experimental. She plans to show some of us off on Visitors' Day. We're to sing on Visitors' Day too, the whole school together, a song called "Scotland the Brave." It's all about mountains and islands and leaping blood. It actually sounds quite good. I'm trying not to hide at the back.

It would be very nice if you could come to hear us.

I have to go now, because it's my turn to collect eggs from the farm, which is a bit mad because the hens are allowed to roam around and you have to try and guess where the eggs are. In Year Nine, we get to kill the hens.

Lots of love, Alice xxx

Little by little, Alice was learning to like school. True, Frau Kirschner's lectures on "Democracy Failing" were a little overwhelming, but there was something gloriously liberating about art classes that always ended up with everyone pretending to be Picts and Romans flinging mud at one another. And while the thought of singing in front of a whole army of parents did terrify her, the music teacher, Senhora Silva, had added Brazilian drums to "Scotland the Brave," and it was impossible not to dance along to them. She still wasn't quite sure about pretending to be French vegetables, but she did love Madoc's classes, and had filled a whole notebook with stories about hares and rabbits.

Alice's pale cheeks were pink now from being outside so much, and they were rounder, too, because like everyone else she was permanently ravenous, and gulped down great bowls of porridge and soup and stew, with hunks of bread and butter and jam, which tasted all the more delicious from knowing they had been grown and raised and made right there in the valley. And though it would be wrong to say that she had become chatty—Alice would probably never be chatty—her silences were becoming more comfortable and less loud. She was on quiet good terms with most of her year, and she was actually friends with Fergus. The giggling in assembly had been followed a few days later by an evening fishing on the dark green loch when Alice, in an unexpected burst of talkativeness, had made up a long story about a drowned world under the water, in which the weeds beneath their boat were the arms of the dead, waving for help. Fergus's blood had frozen as he listened, and later he'd even had a nightmare. He couldn't believe she had made up such a brilliant story.

She couldn't believe she'd actually told it to someone other than Barney, or how much fun it had been to do so. They had become inseparable.

Only two things made Alice sad.

The first was that Jesse wasn't talking to her. She had tried several times to engage him, most recently during the outdoor geography lesson. She had noticed over the past weeks that he was happiest when he was outside, surrounded by nature. Where all the other Year Sevens treated Madoc's class as a holiday, Jesse took it seriously. One day he had asked Madoc a lot of questions about wildlife habitats, and how they were changing, and what could be done about it, and then he had marched off on his own, looking like he knew exactly what he was doing. Alice had followed him, but just as she was going to ask nervously if they could work together, Fergus had come bouncing up.

"Leave him," Fergus had said. "He's still cross because of Captain Fussypants."

To which Alice (who didn't like Fergus's name for Jesse) had replied that *she* didn't call him Captain Fussypants, so why was he cross with her, without understanding how crushed Jesse was by her friendship with Fergus, or how stubborn he was, or how long he could hold a grudge.

0   0   0

The other thing that made her sad was that Barney had not replied to a single one of her emails.

"Is he all right?" she had asked Patience, who had replied that she had no idea—because she had had no news from him either and didn't even know where he was—before adding meanly (partly because he was off doing goodness knew what somewhere in Europe while she was stuck in a poky flat in London, partly because she was cross with him for not writing to Alice), "You know what your father is like."

Which was somewhat contradictory, since one of Patience's main grievances was precisely that Alice didn't know what Barney was like, or at least chose not to admit it.

Which is almost the same thing.

On her third Sunday morning, the day after her latest email to her father, Alice sat on the gate to the pigpen, watching Fergus muck out. Alice liked the pigs, which were fat and pink with great black patches in their long white hair, and she liked the farm, which was tumbledown in exactly the right way, with higgledy stone walls on which a chicken or a goat was always perching, and a garden full of currant bushes that looked like ghosts, swathed in gauze to keep away thieving birds. Today, however, she wasn't looking at any of that but was waving her phone about in an attempt to get some signal — "In case Dad sends a text."

Fergus, who had spent three weeks watching Alice pine for news of Barney and had developed an intense dislike for him, observed that parents were useless.

"Dad's just busy," said Alice, still waving her phone about.

"Well, my parents are useless," Fergus said. "Honestly, sometimes I wonder what it would be like to run away. Properly, I mean, like totally disappearing and national searches and posters and police. Then, when they were fully sobbing, you know, wailing and gnashing teeth, I'd come back and be all, 'Here I am, what appears to be the problem?' That would teach them to get divorced."

She looked at him curiously. "Would it?"

"Probably not," he said lightly. "But quite fun, though. Alice, give up! There's no signal anywhere."

"I just want to talk to him."

This, despite his dislike for Barney, Fergus could understand. Since his parents had separated, he had about a million questions for them. Like, *Why are you splitting up? Why are you going back to Germany? Why do you travel so much? Why can't you take me with you? Why can't I still live at home?*

"What do you want to say to him?" he asked.

"I don't know! Just . . . that I miss him, I suppose."

Fergus was silent for so long, Alice began to worry.

She nudged him.

"I'm just thinking," he said. "There is a place. It's just that we'd be mad to try it."

TWELVE

Kittens!

THE ROOF OF the music tower," said Fergus as they left the pigpen and began to walk back to school. "It's been out of bounds since Carys Middleton fell off it as a twelfth-year."

Alice's eyes widened.

"She used to go up there to call her boyfriend," Fergus explained. "And then they broke up, and she was crying, and she couldn't see. It was OK, because she fell on this ledge, but there was a whole thing because she couldn't get up again and no one found her till morning and she nearly got hypothermia. So now it's kind of forbidden."

"How forbidden?" asked Alice cautiously.

"Totally forbidden." Fergus's eyes began to shine with excitement. "Also totally locked. We'd need to get hold of the key."

Alice looked up toward the music tower, which looked just as sinister as when she had first seen it from the top of the hill, leaning madly to one side, alive with ivy and rooks. More sinister, in fact, because then she had been above it, looking down, whereas now . . .

"I can't."

"We won't get caught, if that's what you're worried about," Fergus assured her. "I mean, we probably won't get caught. And even if we do, what's the worst that can happen? It's not like they're going to expel us. I don't think. They'd make us scrub the tower or paint the windows or something."

He was bouncing with excitement now. Until about a minute and a half ago, he had honestly never given a moment's thought to the music tower roof. Now he couldn't think of anything he wanted more than to climb up onto it. As they drew closer to the school, he could hear the distant caw of the rooks, and it was like they were calling to him — *Come up, come up, it's lovely in the sky!*

"It'll be like your story about the loch," he coaxed. "Except the opposite — a world in the clouds!"

"I can't do it," said Alice, loudly, to sound stronger than she felt, "because it's too high up."

"That's the whole point," said Fergus kindly. "That's why there's a signal."

"I know!" Alice's eyes pricked with tears as she thought of Barney.

"But then—"

"I'm scared of heights!" She hated to admit it. It made her feel weak, and silly, especially when she remembered how unafraid she used to be—her mother's little mountain goat! But there was no getting away from it. Heights were impossible for her. "They turn my legs to jelly."

Fergus stopped walking to stare at her. Alice, afraid! It seemed quite extraordinary to him. He thought about her first morning at school, the way she had hit that reveille gong and brought the whole school out . . . And then he thought about the day she arrived, and the way she had run against Jesse, like she really thought she might beat him . . . And the story she had told him —that story! He still shivered just thinking about it.

"I can't believe you're afraid of anything," he said.

"Well, I am." Alice kicked a pebble down the path. "Heights."

Fergus felt his resolve harden. It wasn't just that he wanted —badly—to go up on the roof. It was because at this moment, Alice looked so small and he didn't like it.

"I'll help you," he said firmly. "I'll hold your hand, if I have to. I've never held hands with a girl before, but I'll do it for you."

He elbowed her in the ribs, to be clear he wasn't being soppy. "Ow!"

"Think of your dad! Think of the phone signal! Think of your phone!"

Alice gulped. She couldn't, she just couldn't.

Could she?

Like Fergus, suddenly what Alice wanted most in the world was to be on the roof of the old tower.

"All right!" she cried as he prepared to elbow her again. "All right! I'll try."

"Excellent!" Fergus beamed. "Then let's get plotting!"

All the way back to school, they thrashed out different ideas.

"The forbidden bit is easy," said Fergus. "We'll just go after dark and make sure nobody sees us. And if they do, we'll say we're doing extra music practice. Teachers love that, when you do extra stuff. So that just leaves the key. There'll be one in the major's study. He has a full set, in a sort of cabinet. I saw it when I . . ."

He stopped.

"What?"

"If you must know, I did once try to run away. But"—he waved toward the vast mountains—"it's not very easy to get away from here. I walked all night, but I only got as far as the car park. Then it started to rain and I sheltered under a bush, and the major found me and brought me back. He was nice. I don't really want to talk about it. Nobody knows except him, and now you. The point is, he has a key."

"Yes!" said Alice, but she couldn't drag her mind away from

thoughts of Fergus, walking alone in the mountains at night. School was one thing, strange but busy and happy and, on the whole, safe. The mountains were different, remote and immovable but at the same time always there and always changing as the wind chased shadows across them and ruffled the bracken and heather.

They were beautiful and scary, and she hadn't made up her mind about them yet. How must it have felt for Fergus to set out alone among them?

"Alice?" Fergus, feeling vulnerable after his admission, was bouncing up and down again. "The major's study? We have to break in."

"Yes!" she repeated, then added, rather obviously, "When he's not there."

"During dinner?"

"But then we're at dinner too."

"You could go first thing in the morning, before reveille — if he turns up, you can say you're . . ."

"What?"

"Muddled? Lost?"

"Sleepwalking?"

"Or just stupid!"

They both cackled with laughter. They were back in the courtyard now, looking up at the major's window.

"Kittens!" Alice said suddenly. "The feeding schedule! That's how we'll get in!"

It was simple. It was genius! To quote Fergus, it was a flipping criminal master plan.

And maybe it was the sun, suddenly shining through a break in the clouds, or maybe it was simply that there are few things in life more thrilling than creating criminal master plans, but they were both suddenly happier and more excited than they could remember ever being. Heads together, voices low, they walked for a long time on the shores of the muddy brown loch, perfecting their plan and fizzing with excitement.

Getting on to the kitten schedule was the easy bit.

"They're horrible," said Jenny, who organized the schedule. "They've got a disgusting litter tray you have to clean, they fight over food, and if you get too close, they bite."

"But they're tiny," Fergus objected.

"There are seven of them," said Jenny darkly. "Whatever you do, do not let them out of the room or you'll never get them back. The vet's coming next week to give them their shots. Hopefully then they'll go outside and get eaten by a fox."

It is not a pleasant thing to talk about, but a litter tray shared by seven cats living together in one small room does not smell nice. That was the first thing Alice and Fergus noticed as they entered the major's study. The second was that there was no sign, anywhere, of the kittens. The third, that there was no sign of the keys.

Fergus swore.

"Which do we look for first? The stinking cats, or the stupid keys?"

A yowl, not dissimilar to the waterpipe noises at Cherry Grange and just as reminiscent of the undead, echoed through the room. The conspirators jumped. Back to back (in a manner akin to Roman soldiers under attack by Picts), they gazed about them. Meowing, scratching, snarling, the kittens came from all directions—the top of a bookshelf, a ceiling lampshade, a curtain rod. They clawed at Alice as she mashed food into bowls. Nipped at Fergus as, gagging, he cleared their litter tray. One of them bolted for the door.

"Why is that open?" shouted Alice.

"I thought you'd closed it!" Fergus screamed, and vanished after the kitten.

Left alone, Alice shakily lined up the feeding bowls. The remaining kittens swarmed forward. One . . . two . . . three . . . four . . . five . . . One was missing!

A faint scratching noise, a pitiful squeak . . . Alice tiptoed round the room, listening. *Scratch* . . . *squeak* . . . the book-case! One of the old-fashioned kind, free-standing, with ancient leather-bound books kept behind glass . . .

Ancient books, and something else . . . She peered closer. A pair of green, marble-round eyes glared back. A tiny pink mouth with sharp little fangs hissed as she reached for the doors; a small furry bullet shot out as she opened them. She ignored it. For at the back of the bookcase was a panel, and on that panel were hooks, and on each hook was a key with a label . . .

Art room, Alice read. *Biology. Chemistry lab.*

Were those footsteps? She rushed to the door. Yes, she could hear voices—one was Fergus, talking unusually loud—a warning . . . She ran back to the bookcase . . .

Dining hall. Entrance hall. French. Geography.

The voices were just outside the door . . . She scanned down the panel for a key labeled *Music* or *Tower* . . .

Neither of them existed. And now the door handle was turning, the speakers were about to come in, their chance was lost! A word was dancing just outside Alice's consciousness, a word she couldn't remember—another name for a castle or a tower —what was it?

"They do wander," she heard the major say. "But well done you for catching him! Now, easy does it—I want to keep the little tykes!"

Keep! That was the word, and there was the key! Alice reached up to unhook it.

When the major and Fergus came into the room, all they saw

was Alice, gently reprimanding a small tabby kitten, smiling like this was the work she was born to do. A few well-chosen words about kittens—"Adorable! So fluffy! No, no, that's not a scratch!" —and the two were off, shoulder to shoulder, swallowing back giggles, the key heavy in Alice's pocket.

Alone in his study, the major scooped up the tabby kitten, deposited it on his shoulder, and looked thoughtfully at the open bookcase.

THIRTEEN

PING!

AT FIRST, ALICE wasn't scared at all. She and Fergus felt their way up the narrow winding staircase of the keep in the dark, and though they held on to the banister rope for safety, she almost didn't need to. The excitement of doing something forbidden, combined with the anticipation of speaking to Barney, had chased all fear of vertigo from her mind. Up they went, past three floors of locked music rooms, passing no one.

A light was on in one of the top-floor rooms. Someone was practicing the violin. Alice and Fergus froze. The violinist kept playing. Holding their breath, they tiptoed onto a short flight of steps at the back of the landing, leading to a bolted, padlocked trapdoor.

The violinist was Jesse, but they didn't know that yet.

Alice opened the padlock, and Fergus slid back the bolt. The trapdoor had been painted over since lovesick Carys's misadventures, and did not open easily. Alice and Fergus thumped away at it as quietly as they could, torn between hysterical laughter and the fear of discovery. When the panel gave way, suddenly, in a cracking and tearing of paint, they clutched the sides of the opening to stop themselves from falling down the stairs, then covered their heads with their arms as a shower of dead leaves poured through the trap and fluttered to the ground around them.

"Messages from the spirits of the sky!" whispered Fergus. "What do you think, Alice? Or the souls of the drowned, finally free of the loch?"

She rolled her eyes and pushed him gently out of the trapdoor ahead of her.

"Oh wow!" he breathed, turning his face to the sky. "Oh wow, oh wow, oh wow!"

Suddenly concerned, he turned back to Alice. "Do you need . . . Should I hold your hand now?"

But Alice had also emerged, and was standing beside him.

She had not imagined, from the ground, how wild it would feel on the roof. On the ground, the wind was barely a whisper, but up here it whooshed and swooped about in gusts and swirls, tugging Alice's hair loose from her braids, whipping her plaid school skirt around her thighs. She tilted her head as Fergus was doing. Heavy gray and white clouds scudded across the sky, carrying the smell of rain, looking close enough to touch.

"Gods, I think," she said, replying to Fergus's earlier questions. "The clouds, I mean. And rain is their way of talking to the world in the loch."

From where she stood, Alice could see the tops of the trees that surrounded the keep, swaying. The rustle of the leaves as they blew back and forth was like the ebb and flow of the sea, the rooks like landlocked gulls, the rooks' nests tossed about like little boats.

It was beautiful. It was magnificent. Everyone, Alice thought dreamily, should spend time on rooftops.

"Have you got any signal yet?"

Fergus's voice brought her back to reality. She pulled her phone out of her pocket and made a face.

"Nothing."

"There's a ledge here. I reckon this must be where Carys fell off."

Not thinking, Alice stepped away from the trapdoor, toward Fergus.

Still not thinking, she looked down.

The lean of the tower was even more pronounced up here, and the roof sloped dramatically away from her toward a parapet, about half a meter tall, on which Fergus was sitting, with nothing but empty space behind him, and a long drop to the ground.

Alice's head began to swim as she wondered how she could have thought this would be all right. Her stomach lurched. She tried to steady her breath.

"Alice, are you OK?"

The ground was so far down! She closed her eyes, feeling the vertigo wash through her in waves. She forced them open then quickly sat down, holding out her phone.

"You look *for* me," she ordered.

Fergus hesitated. Alice's eyes were rolling back, and she was swaying. He could see her knees shaking. If this was what vertigo looked like, he didn't like it. "I think, probably, I should take you back down."

"Please?" She tried to force a smile.

"You look like you're going to faint. Or throw up. Or actually even die."

"I won't die, I promise . . . Just check, quickly."

"What, and if there's a signal you'll call your dad? Alice, you can't even stand!"

Still she held out her phone, even as the nausea rolled on. Silently cursing Barney and his lack of emails, Fergus slipped off the parapet and took the phone, then hoisted himself back up, with his feet dangling over the outside edge. Alice moaned and wrapped her arms around herself.

"Nothing," said Fergus. "Not one single solitary bar. I can try standing up, to see if that works, but only if you can hold on to my jacket. I don't want to fall off like poor old Carys."

"That's not even funny," she croaked.

"I'm not even joking."

Alice shuffled to the edge with her eyes almost completely shut and gripped a fistful of Fergus's uniform as he clambered to his feet, trying not to think about the fact that if he died, it would be her fault.

The wind grew stronger. A gentle rain began to fall.

"Don't slip," she whispered, screwing her eyes shut.

"Believe me, I have no intention of . . ."

PING!

Alice's eyes flew open. A missed call! It must be from Barney — she was sure it must be from Barney — who else could it be?

PING! PING!

Three missed calls!

PING!

"Give me my phone!" She lunged forward. Fergus, caught off guard, took a step back — he wobbled on the edge of the parapet — screamed, and clutched at Alice —

The rooks, disturbed from slumber, took off from their nests in a mass of flapping wings.

PING!

The fifth notification sounded as Alice's phone flew, in a perfect arc, over their heads into the lowering twilight. The pair froze—Alice on the roof clinging to Fergus's legs, Fergus on the parapet gripping her shoulders. For one desperate, hopeful second it looked as if the phone would fall back onto the roof. Fergus let go of Alice with one hand, stretched the other to the sky. But the phone plummeted like a lead weight past him, past the ledge on which the love-struck Carys Middleton had spent a frozen, tearful night, and shattered at the major's feet.

FOURTEEN

We Didn't Mean to Kill You

I F YOU ASKED Jesse privately what he hated most in the world, he would answer without hesitation that it was the violin.

He knew what it was supposed to sound like. In the holidays, his parents had taken him to a concert to hear a violinist famous for playing so fast you couldn't see his bow. Jesse hadn't believed that was physically possible, but it was. Afterwards, his mother had said that was how she imagined angels played in heaven, and his father had added, a little too heartily, "Jesse'll play like that one day," and Jesse had felt depressed because he knew that however hard he tried, he could never play like the man with the angel bow, or even like Jed or Jeremy, who—unlike Jared, who had gone on to play in an orchestra—had given up the violin after the Grade Eight music exam.

Jesse had failed his Grade Five.

Twice.

But he had to try. Trying was what Jesse did.

And so this evening, instead of secretly watching a horror film in the common room with Samira, or fishing on the loch with Jenny and Amir, or playing football with Zeb and most of the other Year Seven boys, Jesse was in his usual practice room right at the top of the keep. His bow, scraping across the strings, sounded like one of the major's trapped kittens, but it didn't matter. One day, he told himself (without much conviction), he would play like a heavenly angel.

He just kept on playing until Alice and Fergus tumbled into the practice room.

Sometimes, when you are interrupted in the middle of doing something, it is very difficult to catch up.

"Hide us!" Fergus hissed.

Jesse paused mid–down-bow.

"Please!" begged Alice.

Jesse lowered his violin. He thought she might be about to cry. "Are you in trouble?"

"Well, duh," said Fergus, peering into a closet. "Why else would we be here? Alice, we can hide in this. Ugh, it's thick with dust—who does the cleaning here? Jesse, play!"

"P-play what?" stammered Jesse.

"What do you think?" Fergus rolled his eyes as he pulled Alice in after him. "Your violin, of course!"

"Thank you," Alice whispered to Jesse, but Fergus had already closed the door.

MEEEOWWW! HISS! SCRATCH! Jesse's hands shook as he dragged his bow across the strings, and he played worse than ever. Inside the closet, Fergus shook with silent laughter.

"He sounds like something dying," he whispered.

"Be nice," Alice said, then, "Fergus, my phone!"

Fergus breathed deeply to try and compose himself.

"It didn't look good," he agreed.

"Did you see who the missed calls were from?"

"It was dark!" he protested. "I was hanging off a roof! Aaaaah . . ."

He sneezed, loudly.

Outside, Jesse's playing paused. They froze. The playing resumed again.

Fergus whimpered as he tried to hold back another sneeze.

"It's the dust!"

"Pinch your nose!" Alice whispered. "Here, I'll do it . . ." She felt for his face in the dark.

"That's my eye!"

"Sorry! Is that your nose?"

"It's my ear!"

"Are you sure you didn't see who the missed calls were from?"

Jesse's playing stopped again.

Discovery took less than a minute.

"Jesse Okuyo!" The major beamed, like Jesse was his favorite person in the world. "Practicing again?"

Jesse mumbled something incoherent.

"Jolly good! Help me out, old chap. I'm looking for a pair of miscreants."

"Miscre . . . whats?"

"Criminals. Wrongdoers." The major lowered his tone to a conspiratorial whisper. "Fugitives from justice. Have you seen any such people?"

"No," croaked Jesse, but his eyes darted to the closet.

"Ah," said the major, and knocked gently on the door.

Out came the miscreants, red-faced and embarrassed and a little bit sneezy. The major beamed again.

"The troublemakers!" he cried. "Luckily unharmed. Unlike this."

Alice gulped as the major held out the remains of her phone.

"The unavoidable consequence, I'm afraid, of throwing a fragile object from a tall building," reflected the major as she took it from him. "Quite beyond repair. Still, it could have been worse. It could have hit me, and then who knows where we'd be? Dead, probably, in my case, and on trial for manslaughter in yours."

"We didn't mean to kill you, sir," Fergus mumbled. "Did we, Alice?"

But Alice could only stare at her phone.

"May I have the key to the roof?" the major enquired genially. "I noticed it was missing. You must learn to anticipate such details, if you are to lead a successful life of crime. Thank you, Mr. Mackenzie. And now, the burning question! What should be the Consequence of all this misbehavior? In the ancient world, they would cut off the hands of thieves—don't look so panicked, Mr. Okuyo! Of course I am not going to do that. Now, let me think . . ."

They watched nervously, flattened against the wall, as he paced the practice room, filling the small space with his massive frame.

"I have it!" They all jumped as he clapped his hands. "The perfect Consequence! I am putting all three of you together as a team on the Great Orienteering Challenge!"

"But I didn't do anything wrong!" cried Jesse.

The major's eye was suddenly icy. "I believe you lied to me, Mr. Okuyo."

Jesse blushed and stared at the ground.

"It is a perfect Consequence," the major repeated. "Possibly my best ever. Now, I spot a piano. It has been an age since I practiced. Off you go, to other pursuits. I understand there is a highly illegal film being shown in the Year Seven common room. Failing that, you could attempt to catch a fish. I shall play

Rachmaninov." He cracked the joints in his fingers. "What are you waiting for? Go!"

They left, to a torrent of musical notes.

Jesse ran down the winding staircase, heedless of the steep, slippery steps. He was furious. The Orienteering Challenge! The one thing he had been looking forward to this term! Fergus was going to ruin it for him—Jesse knew he was! Fergus always ruined everything.

Fergus followed at a more leisurely pace, astounded at having got off so lightly. Alice followed, cradling her phone.

The major smiled. He had rarely felt so pleased with himself. He had set something in motion with this Consequence. He looked forward to finding out what it was.

Somewhere in a different country, Barney Mistlethwaite once again tried to call his daughter. He had an urgent message to give her.

FIFTEEN

Like a Swamp,
Without the Crocodiles

THE FIRST TRAINING exercise for the Great Orienteering Challenge took place the following Saturday morning. Madoc, who was in charge on the basis that he taught geography and therefore knew about maps, gathered the Year Sevens in the Great Hall after breakfast to give them their instructions.

"Today you will be playing Capture the Flag," he told them. "There are three flags planted in three different locations in the surrounding countryside. You will be divided into three groups, which in turn will be divided into teams, each of which will be given the coordinates of one of the flags. The first team in each group to bring back their flag are the winners. Are there any questions?"

"What are coordinates, sir?" asked Duffy.

Madoc, who had been practicing map coordinates with his

students since the beginning of the year, began to feel apprehensive.

"Does anyone remember?" he asked.

Jesse's hand shot up.

"A map coordinate refers to the latitude and longitude of a position," he recited. "Longitude lines are perpendicular to the equator, and latitude lines are parallel. A geographic coordinate system enables every location on Earth to be specified by a set of numbers, letters, or symbols."

"Excellent, Jesse! I'm glad someone in class was listening."

Jesse blushed under the unaccustomed praise. Madoc, feeling a little more hopeful, told the students to pick up their Orienteering Survival Packs on their way out. "You'll find maps and compasses, water and packed lunches. Orange waterproofs are hanging by the door and are to be worn at all times. I repeat, at all times. Even if it isn't raining."

"In case we get lost," Jenny explained to Alice, who was looking mystified. "So they can find us easily before we die of exposure."

"People do get lost, all the time," Samira added. "And last year someone broke a leg. They had to send a helicopter. Orienteering's a lot harder than you think."

Alice, alarmed, glanced at Jesse. This time, when she caught his eye, he didn't look away, but shook his head with a little smile, like he was telling her to ignore Jenny and Samira, and that everything would be fine. Alice smiled back, relieved. Fergus, watching, felt a stab of jealousy.

The sun was out again after a week of rain, and a playful breeze scooted high clouds across a pale blue sky. Despite his misgivings about having Fergus on the team, Jesse was in high spirits. In the week since the incident in the music tower, he had thought a lot about what to do about today's training exercise. His first idea had been to beg the major to put him and Fergus on different teams, but he was almost one hundred percent sure that wouldn't work. Instead, he had emailed Jared (the least annoying of his brothers) for advice.

Jared's answer had been clear. *Be the boss, little brother. Take control.*

It was what the knights in his stories would have done too.

The moment Madoc handed out the coordinates, Jesse became bossier than he had ever dreamed he could be. He would plan their route, he declared—the other two just needed to follow him. He studied the map in silence while they waited, then nodded and put it in his pocket. There was an obvious way to go, he said, which the other groups were sure to take. He, Jesse, could do better.

"Ready, steady, go!" As soon as Madoc declared the exercise started, Jesse hurried Alice and Fergus through the griffin gates ahead of all the other teams. Then, as soon as they came to the first hairpin bend, he pulled them behind a rhododendron bush.

"What?" Fergus protested. "That hurt!"

"Shortcut!" Jesse whispered.

They crept after him through the trees, a thick carpet of pine needles muffling their footsteps.

A little farther into the undergrowth, they came to a path, just wide enough for one, winding through a pine wood. Jesse checked off landmarks as they went—an abandoned cottage, a pond, the brook that fed it. They were walking north by northeast, exactly as he'd planned. He felt a rush of exhilaration. Maps for Jesse held the same power as stories held for Alice. He read them the way most people read books, seeing an actual landscape where his classmates saw only lines on paper. He loved how maps changed the way he looked at the world around him. As he searched for clues to confirm their location, he saw so much that he would otherwise have missed: a tiny bird's nest, a badger sett, a caterpillar . . .

He held up his hand to stop the others.

"What now?"

"Up there, on that branch!"

Alice gasped, delighted.

Tufty ears and eyes like black marbles, a plume of a tail and a nut-brown body, four small paws clinging to the trunk of a pine tree, head pointing toward them, nose and whiskers twitching . . .

The prettiest thing she had ever seen.

"A red squirrel," Jesse whispered. "You don't get them in the south. Hardly ever, anyway, but they still exist in Scotland."

A memory stirred deep inside Alice. Not an actual squirrel, but a picture book, read with her mother in the garden at Cherry Grange, and Mum saying, *We used to have a pair in the garden when I was a little girl in Poland. They were so tame they used to steal things from the table when we ate outside.* Alice had eaten every single meal outside for weeks after that in the hope of seeing a red squirrel of her own. For a fleeting moment, her mother was there in the woods with them, dancing on the grass in the garden, her long dark hair lifted in the breeze, laughing and singing, *Dance with me, little pigeon.*

Little pigeon had been another of her special names for Alice.

Alice blinked. When she looked again, her mother was gone, but the squirrel was still there, staring straight at her with its marble eyes, as if her mother had sent it.

For the first time since smashing her phone, Alice smiled.

Fergus felt another stab of jealousy.

Like a lot of very smart people, Fergus saw nothing extraordinary in his own gifts. Instead, though he would never have admitted it, he envied Jesse what he didn't have himself—his good looks, his gentle kindness, his physical strength. He envied him his family, the serene parents who always seemed so happy together. He even envied Jesse the merciless, teasing brothers, who all descended on the school in a loud noisy group every Visitors' Day, forever hugging and cuffing their youngest sibling with real affection.

The only family Fergus had was his parents, and they never came to Visitors' Day, because they might see each other.

He'd dealt with his envy in the past by laughing at Jesse for his stuffiness over school rules, but today was different. Today, Captain Fussypants was behaving like someone in charge, and Alice couldn't stop smiling at him.

Alice was Fergus's friend. She had no business smiling at Jesse all the time.

"I thought we were in a hurry," he said loudly.

The squirrel, startled, pounced. For a few seconds, as it flew across the path high above them, they saw it outlined in full flight against a patch of sky. Then it landed and disappeared, a few swaying branches the only sign that it had ever been there. Still Alice stood, rooted to the spot, hoping for another glimpse, while Jesse waited and clever Fergus marched on ahead, blood boiling, ready to do something really, really stupid.

The path widened as they came out of the wood, tracing a wide loop around a lush green meadow dotted with yellow flowers. Jesse stopped to show them the map.

"We follow the path round the meadow," he said, "then we start to climb — these circular lines close together mean it's quite a steep hill — and then on the other side there's a valley, and that is where the flag is."

"Says who?" asked Fergus.

Jesse frowned. "Says the map."

A little voice at the back of his mind told Fergus he was being an idiot, but he didn't listen.

"I think, if you want to save time, you should just walk across the meadow," he announced. "I think the map's wrong."

Jesse looked appalled. "The map is never wrong!"

But there was no reasoning with Fergus in this sort of mood. He looked wild and mutinous. Alice realized with alarm that he was also enjoying it.

"Let's have a race!" he shouted, and took off at a sprint across the meadow.

"Fergus, don't!" Jesse shouted. "Fergus, come back!"

But Fergus was already running.

He got halfway across the meadow before his feet sank straight into the ground.

"What's happening?" cried Alice.

"It's a bog," Jesse said grimly. "And he's stuck."

"A bog?"

"Like a swamp, without the crocodiles. People drown in them."

Alice took off at a run.

"Come back! Alice! Oh, for— ALICE, WAIT!"

"We have to rescue him!" she shouted, and sank, without warning, up to her knees in mud.

WHOOSH! Jesse, running up behind her, lifted her clear and threw her, then himself, to the ground.

"We have to distribute our weight so there's less chance of sinking," he explained. "Otherwise we'll all get stuck, and then—"

"It's over my knees!" wailed Fergus, flailing around.

"Just stop moving!" Jesse shouted. "I'm coming!"

"And then what?" asked Alice.

"Then, I guess, unless they find us—we all die. Now, can you drag yourself back to the path? Please? While I help Fergus?"

Flat on her belly, she slithered across the stinking bog, freezing mud seeping in through the collar and cuffs of her weatherproof clothing, until she felt dry ground beneath her. Breathlessly, she watched as Jesse slithered toward Fergus—as Fergus stopped thrashing about and listened, then started to slowly, slowly raise one leg clear and take a step backwards, and then the other leg —as he fell flat, like Jesse, and with Jesse dragged himself back to the path, where he collapsed, panting.

"And that," said Jesse, "is why you need to do exactly what I say."

SIXTEEN

Kings and Queen

W E'RE GOING ON," said Jesse sternly, when Fergus was able to speak again and had asked if they could go home, because he didn't feel very well.

"It's very cold," Alice ventured.

Be the boss, Jesse reminded himself as he tried to stop his own teeth from chattering.

"You'll warm up when you start walking," he said. "And Fergus is fine. Now, shut up, both of you, while I try to make up time."

Damp, muddy, shame-faced, and bedraggled, their clothes steaming gently in the sun, Alice and Fergus sat meekly on boulders eating soggy, only slightly muddy sandwiches while Jesse studied the map.

"There's another shortcut," he announced. "See this path here? I reckon if we cut out this loop and climb up these rocks—they're quite steep—we should shave off twenty minutes."

At the mention of the steep rocks, Fergus glanced at Alice. She stuck her chin forward and refused to look at him. Instead, jumping to her feet, she pulled her map from the plastic wallet hanging round her neck and produced a compass from her pocket. This was her chance, she decided, to show Jesse that she wanted to be his friend and that the First Day Challenge was forgotten.

It was not the moment for vertigo.

"This way," she announced, and set off in the wrong direction.

Jesse sighed, reached for her map, turned it the right way up, and pointed the other way.

"Are you sure?" she asked.

He rounded his eyes. "The compass never lies."

Jesse had been right; the rocks were steep. But Alice, by breathing deeply and looking straight ahead, was fine. She may have started to cry at one point, and they may have had to hold her hand, and she may have begged them to go ahead without her and leave her to die. And Jesse may have lost his temper and said you could only win if the whole team came back, so she had better not die. And Fergus may have made a sarcastic remark about Jesse's excellent and sympathetic leadership, which may have led to Jesse shouting again. But they made it. And when they reached the top—which was flat, and wide enough for the ground to feel good and firm beneath Alice's feet, and had splendid three-hundred-and-sixty-degree views of the mountains—well, it was absolutely worth it, because the world was at their feet and they felt like its kings and queen.

Far below them, planted in a mound of grass, the unclaimed blue and white school flag fluttered, but Jesse made no move toward it. Instead, he pulled binoculars from his pocket to watch an eagle flying overhead, before passing them to Alice.

You could be a hero in a place like this, he thought.

It was Alice who saw through the binoculars the other team coming from the north (or the east—she wasn't quite sure), marching across the flat land, making slow but steady progress toward the flag.

"Jesse!" she screamed. "RUN!"

And oh, how he ran! Tumbling down the hill, sprinting through the heather, leaping over brooks, his mud-streaked jacket billowing behind him. The other team spotted him and began to run too, but they stood no chance against Jesse, now bounding gazelle-like toward his prize.

He plucked it from the ground and waved it in the air, then, because he was too excited to be tired, ran back toward the others, who were tearing down toward him, and they all hugged and high-fived and punched each other, screaming, "We won we won we won!"

How nice, when happiness is simple.

Schoolwards they returned—filthy, smelly, sweaty, with blisters forming where their damp socks rubbed their heels, but happy, because they had won, and the universe was on their side.

The loch was purple today, with playful amethyst waves. Alice stopped to admire it, then tramped up the stairs to her room, leaving a trail of dried mud behind her. She was going to have a shower and wash every millimeter of dirt from her body, and then she was going to go down to tea and eat as many cakes and buns as she physically could, and then there were more vegetables to study for French, and some math problems, and after dinner (where she was sure she could eat a horse) she would watch a film with Samira, or visit some new piglets with Fergus, or just read a book. All of which were good options.

For the first time since she'd arrived, she realized there was nowhere else she wanted to be.

Which all goes to show that the universe has a pretty ironic sense of timing, because when she finally reached her room, there was a letter from Barney, waiting on her desk.

SEVENTEEN

The Lake Isle of Innisfree

R OME, 10 MAY

Alicat!

How goes Scotland? Is it raining? I remember it always rains!

Guess what? I'm coming to see you! Auntie P says she's going to a gig called Visitors' Day, and I'm coming with her! I'm already polishing my shoes! (Joke—you know I always wear sneakers!)

Be good, Alicat—and if you can't be good, don't get caught!

Kisses,

Dad

P.S. You should be receiving a parcel from Italy soon. Don't open it! It's a secret!

It was not, in any way, a satisfying letter. In fact, it wasn't a letter at all but a postcard, with Barney's short message on one side and a picture of a great big naked statue peeing into a fountain on the other. The postcard had been stamped and addressed and then, inexplicably, posted in an envelope with another stamp. Alice read it twice, then stared at the picture, as if the peeing statue might contain some hidden message she couldn't understand.

It didn't.

Barney, at Stormy Loch, for Visitors' Day! In just under a week, he would be here, and she could show him everything—her little room, the farm, the keep, the castle . . . She could take him to Madoc's field, where she had counted hares and rabbits; they could look for red squirrels; they could go boating on the loch . . . She could introduce him to her friends . . .

So why was she not dancing about the room?

Perhaps if the postcard had not come today, when she was so happy . . . Perhaps if his message were not so short compared to her own long, chatty emails and if he had remembered that Alice had also mentioned Visitors' Day to him, many times— perhaps then she could have been over the moon. As it was, she was just . . . confused.

She tucked the postcard into her notebook and laid the notebook neatly right in the middle of her desk. Then, still in her muddy clothes, she sat down and stared at it . . . opened it, read a few lines of her latest story, about the drowned village in the loch . . . picked up a pencil and tried to write, but gave up when no words came.

Barney, at Stormy Loch!

She didn't know what to think.

The parcel from Italy arrived the following day by registered mail, a small yellow padded mailer tightly bound with brown tape. She took it to her room and lay with it on her bed, trying to guess what was inside. Barney had brought many presents back from his travels—lace fans from Seville and elephant carvings from Kenya, Indian puppets, Italian sweets . . . She wondered what this one could be. The parcel weighed about the same as a short hardback book, and it was squishy, like bubble wrap, but inside the squishiness she felt something like a small square box. She almost opened it—angry, suddenly, at the secrecy and the short letter. She went as far as asking Jenny in the room next door for some scissors and slid them beneath the brown tape —but stopped.

It's a secret, he had written, and she didn't want to spoil the surprise.

She put the parcel away in the drawer of her desk and tried to forget about it.

Which, on the one hand, was a shame. Opening it could have avoided a lot of heartache. And danger, and betrayal, and the near-death experiences I've already mentioned.

On the other hand, opening it would have turned this into a very different story.

The weather was gloriously sunny for all of the week leading up to Visitors' Day. More and more teachers moved their classes outside, with Madoc organizing dawn hikes to the mouth of the valley to search for orchids, and Mr. Busby, the biology teacher, leading pupils to the shallow end of the sparkling blue loch to look for newts. The major, ever optimistic, decided that Visitors' Day should take place outdoors. A tent went up for the picnic lunch and tea, an outdoor stage was erected for the entertainment. Rehearsals for the blue-painted "Democracy Failing" and the rendition of "Scotland the Brave" with its extra Brazilian drums were moved to the rose garden, which overnight had burst into bloom and color. Professor Lawrence, the chemistry teacher, who had been perfecting her daytime fireworks, rowed out to the middle of the loch for a practice run and let off three flares that traced perfect arcs of pink, orange, and green against the bright blue sky. To the Year Sevens, who had no summer exams, it felt like a holiday, yet still Alice could not shake off the feelings provoked by Barney's letter.

On a baking Wednesday afternoon, Dr. Csintalan, who taught literature, took to the loch with the Year Sevens for a poetry class.

They set out in a flotilla of rowboats, with swallows dipping in and out of the water around them, right into the middle of the loch, where they formed a floating island, the prows of their boats touching, each craft secured to the next by students holding oars, and Dr. Csintalan announced, "I will now recite a poem! 'The Lake Isle of Innisfree,' by Irish genius W. B. Yeats!"

"What, here, sir?" asked Zeb.

"Yes, here! You will see how appropriate it is! Now, pay attention! I shall attempt to project my voice, but it is not so easy when one is wobbling about on water."

Poetry was serious business to Dr. Csintalan, who had been raised by Hungarian immigrant parents on a steady diet of English classics. He stood up in the little rowboat and, eyes closed, head thrown back, struck a dramatic pose. The students stared. Fergus nudged Jesse. "Rock the boat," he mouthed. Jesse, who liked Fergus better since they had won the orienteering exercise but still did not approve of him, said no. Dr. Csintalan opened his eyes and began.

"'I will arise and go now, and go to Innisfree . . .'"

It was a lovely poem, about a poet who wanted to go to an island in a lake and build a cabin and grow beans and keep bees and listen to birds and crickets. Alice listened, entranced, as Dr. Csintalan recited it from memory without once faltering.

> *I hear lake water lapping with low sounds by the shore*
> *While I stand on the roadway, or on the pavements grey,*
> *I hear it in the deep heart's core.*

Dr. Csintalan finished reciting and gazed at the loch and the mountains as if he had never seen them before. "'I hear it in the deep heart's core,'" he murmured. "Is there a more beautiful line in poetry? Yeats wrote this poem when he was in London, far from home, about an island in a lake that he loved. 'I hear it in the deep heart's core'—the idea that our heart is trying to tell us something, if only we would stop and listen . . ."

He saw Alice watching and smiled.

"Homework! Five hundred words on the deep heart's core and what you hear when you listen to it. Yeats's poem is about longing—for home, for beauty, above all for peace. What do you long for?"

Someone said, "No more homework, ever," and everybody laughed.

"No, no," said Dr. Csintalan. "I am not asking what do you want. I am asking what do you long for?"

Alice looked around at her pensive classmates and tried to guess their answers. She knew, for example, that Samira had a sister who was very ill in hospital. If Alice were Samira, what she would long for more than anything was for her sister to be better. And Duffy—how many times had she heard him rage against being so small? She could perfectly imagine him longing to be tall. She knew that Fergus, though he never spoke about it, longed for his parents to be back together, and she had guessed long ago that Jesse yearned for a talent he could be proud of . . .

What did she long for?

Fergus, who could never be serious for long, suddenly yelled, "Water fight!" and splashed Zeb with his oar. Zeb leaned out to splash Fergus and accidentally on purpose fell into the loch, and then Duffy got overexcited and jumped in, and someone pushed Esme in, until the whole class was bobbing about in the water, including Dr. Csintalan, and Alice forgot the question in the general mayhem and happiness. But later, doing her homework, she sat at her desk and stared for a long time at what she had written.

Once there was an old house in a garden full of trees, where a little girl lived with her family. Her mother would

tell her stories every evening, and sometimes when it rained
they would bake together, using a book of family recipes
her mother had brought with her when she left her country.
The little girl had a bedroom from which in the summer
she could pick cherries, and the whole top floor was attics
where her aunt could paint, and her father made her a
swing, and people loved her, and she felt safe.

What I want most in my deep heart's core is . . .

She stared and stared, but she had no idea what she longed
for. She only knew that she wanted it so much it hurt.

EIGHTEEN

Baby Birds and Kittens and Other Waifs

ON THE NIGHT before Visitors' Day, Alice had a nightmare. It was one she had had many times since her mother died, and it was a memory as much as a dream. A few days after her mother's funeral, she had woken in the middle of the night and run down the landing to Barney's room, only to find that he had gone away. Aunt Patience, trying to comfort her, had said it was just for a few days. To grieving seven-year-old Alice, those few days had felt like years. She had dreamed of the empty hallway every night until his return, and she still dreamed of it now whenever he was away or due to come back.

She woke in a cold sweat in the small hours on Visitors' Day and did not sleep again. The dread of the nightmare stayed with her through breakfast. Each in his way, Jesse and Fergus tried to look after her. Jesse, knowing little about Barney, heaped her plate with food. Fergus, knowing more, tried to distract her with jokes.

She did not eat. She did not laugh. She talked even less than usual.

The students cleared breakfast, swept the dining hall, made their beds and tidied their rooms, put up bunting in the picnic tent and flower garlands on the outdoor stage. At eleven o'clock, the first bus arrived, bringing visitors from the bottom of the hill. The first parents came out. Duffy's dad, small and sturdy like his son . . . Tatiana's mother, wrapped in fur . . . Jesse's mum, smooth and golden in pale tweed, his dad, dark and handsome in a navy blazer, his laughing, joking brothers . . .

The second bus came. Jenny's jolly mother appeared, then Samira's parents, with a very thin, very frail little girl beaming from ear to ear . . . The flash of apple-green coat—Aunt Patience! Alice's heart soared with hope.

Then crashed, when no one else came out.

She had hoped so hard that this time would be different.

The clement weather had vanished overnight, leaving the day's organizers gazing anxiously at the sky. Under lowering clouds, Patience and Alice walked away from the castle toward the loch.

"I don't know what happened," Patience said. "He arrived yesterday at my flat, and we were going to fly to Edinburgh together.

But then just before we were due to leave, he went out. I haven't heard a squeak from him since, except a short message to say there had been a change of plan. Oh, Alice!"

They had reached the water, which today was dark and choppy and bleakly beautiful. Patience stood on the shore, reaching her arms out to the view as if she were trying to hug it. "I wish I could paint this!"

Alice, at this moment, couldn't have cared less about the loch.

"Did Dad give you a message for me?" she asked.

"Of course he did!" Patience lied. "He sends heaps of love, and says he's really sorry." She came away from the loch and took her niece's hands. "Darling, you do like it here, don't you?"

"I miss home."

The words, spoken out loud, delivered their truth to Alice like a punch in the stomach. She loved it here, but it wasn't enough. She didn't think anywhere would ever be enough.

Patience put her arms around her. "Oh, darling."

"And I want Mum."

They sat for a while in silence while Patience considered her reply.

"Do you remember," she said at last, "once, when you were little, you climbed out of your bedroom window to sleep in the cherry tree?"

Alice shook her head.

"Well, you did, and then you were furious when your mother ordered you to come back in. You shouted and cried that you wanted to sleep among the cherry blossoms like a princess. When your mum finally did manage to bribe you back in with the promise of ice cream, you wouldn't talk to her, just took the ice cream and closed the door in her face. She'd locked your window by then, of course, like any sensible mother. But do you know what she said to me that night? She laughed, and said she hoped you would always be fearless and want to sleep among cherry blossoms. She was already ill then. I think she was trying to be fearless too."

Alice looked away so her aunt wouldn't see her trying not to cry.

"I want what she wanted, darling. For you to be fearless, like you used to be. To climb out of windows, and up trees, and to live life, the way she did. Dancing in the garden—do you remember?"

Alice gave a tiny nod. Patience squeezed her hand.

"Stories end, darling, and that's sad, but they have to so new ones can begin. It's why I sent you here. Someone—a friend —had told me about this school, and Major Fortescue. She— my friend—said it was a place that was good for people starting again. And I don't think Cherry Grange was good for us anymore, darling. Too much history, when we should be looking to the future. I think the dear old house was hurting us."

She didn't add the other things her friend had told her — that the major was famous for collecting waifs and strays, or that he only ever asked people to pay what they could afford, which in Patience's case, even with the sale of the house, was not much. And when Alice asked, after a long silence, "Where was Dad, that night when I climbed out of the tree?" she bit her tongue and only answered, "Somewhere around, I expect, I don't remember," instead of the truth, which was that even when Alice's mother was alive, no one ever really knew what Barney was up to.

The heavens opened as they walked back. Stormy Loch took it on the chin. The concert was moved into the Great Hall; the fireworks display was put off to another day. The picnic tent collapsed and cakes were demolished with gusto in the dining hall instead. The rain washed away the paint of "Democracy Failing," causing the students to cheer and Frau Kirschner to resign in disgust. The day was happily declared a triumph.

Alice sang with the others and pecked at a cake, but Patience could see that her heart wasn't in it. They did not talk about Alice's parents again, but before she left, Patience took a small flat parcel from her bag and gave it to her niece.

"Open it," she said.

It was an exquisite, delicate watercolor of a spray of white roses.

"Even in the pot, they flowered," she said. "I wanted to bring you some, but I was worried they wouldn't survive the journey."

A lump rose to Alice's throat. Patience pulled her into another hug.

"Fearless," she whispered. "Don't forget."

Away the visitors went again, huddling under umbrellas to the buses, waving and blowing kisses. Tatiana waltzed past, all smiles. "Nice to see your brothers, Jesse! I am definitely taking them out in my Maserati when I win that million. Funny"—she laughed—"you look smaller next to them."

Jesse scowled.

"Cheer up," said Fergus. "At least your family came."

He spoke lightly, but not enough to disguise his bitterness. Alice briefly dragged her thoughts away from her own unhappiness.

"I'm sorry they didn't come, Fer."

"Ah, don't be! I told you they were useless. You OK, Alice?"

"I think I'm going to go to bed."

"But it's not even five o'clock! What about dinner?"

"I'm not hungry."

Fergus watched her go, worried. He had been furious with Barney for not coming—much more than with his own parents.

He had never expected them, but he knew how hard Alice had been hoping.

While the rest of the school were clearing up after Visitors' Day, Fergus sneaked away to the library and typed *Barney Mistlethwaite* into the search engine. A short Wikipedia entry came up, listing a handful of plays, a TV series, and a couple of films, all a long time ago. So who was Barney Mistlethwaite? He wandered on to Barney's personal bio—one sister, Patience, a painter. A daughter, Alice, of course. A wife, Clara Mistlethwaite, born Kaminska, deceased . . .

The eye sees what the heart desires, the therapist his parents had sent him to after they separated had said. Fergus knew this to be true—he just wondered what it was Alice desired. Feeling pensive, he deleted his browsing history and closed down the computer.

There was a lot more he could have found out about Barney Mistlethwaite, if he'd searched a little harder—none of it to do with acting. Still, what you don't know won't kill you—that was another one of the therapist's sayings.

Except, of course, when it nearly does.

NINETEEN

Stormy Loch

ALICE WENT UP to her room and climbed into bed and tried to think only good things about Barney, like the swing he had made and hung in the old oak tree at home, and his big warm laugh and excellent hugs. She tried to convince herself that these were the things that mattered, much more than forgetting her at school when she was little, and not answering her emails, and failing to turn up at a moment's notice. She tried not to count how many times he had not turned up before.

Sitting up against her pillows, she traced the contours of her aunt's watercolor roses, and in her imagination the painting grew and grew, until its thorny branches burst out of the frame and filled her little room. She closed her eyes to chase them away and saw her mother again, dancing in the garden. Blinked, and saw the empty hallway of her dream.

She pushed away the duvet and went over to the window. Outside, the rain had stopped and a weak sun threw a pale path across the dark waters of the loch. She opened the window and leaned out, breathing in great gulps of clean, damp air.

Now, in her mind, she heard Dr. Csintalan ask his question —What do you long for in your deep heart's core?—and suddenly she knew the answer.

She wanted to be the girl Patience had told her about. The princess in the cherry blossoms. Her mother's fearless climber.

She closed her window again and ran out to the loch.

She could not tell them afterwards why she had done what she did, except that she wanted to be brave, and the loch was there, and the sun was shining a path on it like something in a story.

For a while, just looking at it was enough. But only for a while.

The boathouse was built on stilts over the water, with floating platforms running along the walls and a jetty down the middle that wobbled as Alice walked along it. For a few seconds, as she stumbled and fought to regain her balance, she looked straight down and saw her own reflection in the coal-black water, and thought of the drowned world. Upright again, she banished these thoughts and walked firmly to the farthest boat, untied the painter, climbed in, clambered over a crate, picked up the oars, and rowed out.

At first, Alice felt magnificent, as though the world existed only for her, but when the sun disappeared behind a cloud, she woke from her sunlit trance in the middle of a loch that was not gold but dark gunmetal gray, and she was cold and exhausted with hands covered in blisters from the rowing. She turned the boat and began to row back, but now the wind was against her, and she was going against the current. One of her blisters burst and started to bleed. She dropped an oar. Then, as she tried to retrieve it, she dropped the other one.

The weeds swayed beneath her like people waving.

Feeling anything but fearless, Alice tried to shout for help. Bracing her feet against the sides of the boat, she stood and yelled through cupped hands, but it was pointless. She was half a kilometer across a loch, and everyone else was indoors. Nobody saw or heard a thing.

She only realized when she sat down again what cargo she was carrying.

The crate in the bottom of the boat contained Professor Lawrence's fireworks and a lighter.

Please never, ever try at home what Alice did next.

We have to assume that, being an intelligent girl, she was

too tired to think straight. Or too frightened to know any better. Either way, she was lucky that the fireworks, even in their crate, had suffered from the damp, and didn't all go up when she lit the taper. The roman candles, the Catherine wheels, the rockets all fizzled damply in their shells and decided, on balance, that they would rather not ignite. But the flares—ah, the flares! Professor Lawrence, rushing to the window with the rest of the school when the shout went up, felt a glow of professional pride. Fuchsia pink, emerald green, and bright orange, punctuated by showers of silver stars—the flares were magnificent.

"Is it the Northern Lights?" breathed a small pink girl.

"No, Daphne." The professor sighed. "It's science."

Stormy Loch was an unconventional school, with an approximate approach to health and safety, but they knew the basics. Which is to say, they had a motorboat, and they knew how to use it.

Madoc drove the boat, Matron behind him at the ready with a first-aid kit, the major at his side with his binoculars. Over the dark water and the golden wavelets they sped, toward the little rowboat drifting now on the far side of the loch.

The little rowboat that appeared to be . . . empty.

Madoc cut the engine and steered carefully toward it. The major caught it and pulled them to. Their hearts in their mouths, they peered over the edge. Perhaps the rower had fainted—or was hiding.

But there was no one in the rowboat.

Alice, suddenly alive to the danger of live fireworks, had done the only sensible thing and jumped into the loch.

TWENTY

Midnight Picnics

S HE WOKE IN the infirmary, with the major at her bedside. "Ah good," he said. "You're awake. You've been asleep a very long time."

She looked toward the window and saw that it was light outside. "What is the time?" she asked.

"About two o'clock in the afternoon. You've slept almost around the clock. Quite the fright you gave us, I must say. You were clinging to the side of the boat when we found you, and you fainted when we plucked you from the water. It's been a dramatic day, one way and another — the weather, the tent, Frau Kirschner's resignation . . . But really, in the drama stakes, you take first prize."

Alice, feeling mortified, mumbled an apology.

"I fancy myself a good judge of character, Miss Mistlethwaite," the major mused. "And yet I confess myself a little baffled by yours. What do you say?"

He peered at her with his good eye.

"I don't know . . . I mean, I don't know what you think about me, or my character."

He sat back in his chair, resting his chin on his hands.

"It seems to me," he explained, "that since you arrived here, your behavior has been, shall we say, erratic. On the one hand, you have made friends. You have joined in. Your teachers tell me that, bar a pronounced tendency to daydream, you work well in class. On the other hand . . ."

He performed a sort of royal wave, as if to imply that the other hand, comprising as it did rooftops, gongs, explosions, and near drownings, was too exhausting to detail.

"I never used to do mad things," she told him. "At home, I mean. All I did was read and write stories. It's just, since I've been here . . ."

"Yes?"

How could she explain—the sense of vastness from the moment she stepped off the train at Castlehaig, that first morning hammering the gong in the silent hall, the sky on the roof of the keep, the feeling of being a queen with the world at her feet, the sun path on the loch . . .

"It's like stories come alive here," she said. "And it's so big. I think it makes me want to be big too."

The major nodded, looking pleased, then asked curiously, "What were you thinking when you took the boat out on the loch, alone and without informing anyone, in such terrible conditions?"

"That I was in a story," Alice admitted, feeling even more mortified. "And that I wanted to do something brave."

"Ah," said the major. "Something brave."

He closed his eye, thinking—as he quite frequently did—that children were fascinating but also exhausting, and he stayed like this for so long that Alice thought he might have fallen asleep. She was just wondering if it would be acceptable to poke him when he stirred and asked, "Were you afraid?"

"Not when I set out," she replied. "Only later, when I thought I couldn't get back."

There was another pause, and then, "I am not sure you can be brave, if you are not afraid," the major said. "Being brave means standing up to the things that frighten us, even as we are quaking in our boots. There is so much in this world that is utterly bewildering. Jumping into lochs, dancing about on rooftops—these things may be reckless, or joyous, or dangerous, but I do not think they are courageous. To be fearless, we must first banish our fears, and to achieve that, we must look them in the face."

He smiled, seeing how hard she was trying to understand him.

"However! There is more to life than fear and bewilderment. Sometimes the beauty of the world can take your breath away — just wait for the Orienteering Challenge and you will see what I mean. And the summer nights — the wonderful northern summer nights! Soon they will be so short it will be almost always daylight. Students will sneak out for midnight picnics while the staff pretend not to notice . . . Dr. Csintalan will row on the lake in the small hours of the morning composing poetry, and who knows? Perhaps Mr. Madoc will find love again. We must take care of the beauty in the world, Miss Mistlethwaite. It is one of the reasons I started the school here, in this valley. We must look after it — but perhaps we may also enjoy it? Perhaps . . . you could try to enjoy it?"

It was a tempting proposition, especially to a girl who in the past day had almost drowned, nearly blown herself up, and been sorely disappointed by her only parent. But there was one last thing, and if Alice was to face up to her fears, she knew that she had to ask.

"Sir, shouldn't there be Consequences? Melanie, the girl who had my room before — she was expelled for blowing up the chemistry lab. Isn't this just as bad?"

"Oh, I don't think so," said the major. "A bit of a scare, but no harm done. This is your home, after all. I think we'll give you one more chance."

Alice felt immeasurable relief. The major stood with a great creaking of bones and pressed his giant hand on top of her head in a kind of gentle blessing. "But perhaps try to keep out of trouble until the end of term?"

He smiled, so benevolently it was impossible not to smile back.

"I promise," she said.

"Excellent! And meanwhile, perhaps things are not as bleak as you imagine them."

He left. Alice sank back into her pillow. She wondered what he could possibly mean, then forgot about it, lulled by the surprising softness of her infirmary bed, the crisp linen, the smell of lavender. Unlike the rest of the castle, this room was neat as a pin, freshly painted white, with gleaming floorboards and clean windows through which she could see the tops of trees. She felt safe, and cosseted. An improbable lightness began to bubble up inside her. There were things she was afraid of, and one day she would face them and become fearless. But in the meantime, midnight picnics sounded fun, and white nights. She could already feel the stirrings of a new story, a happy one, about a family of hares driven from their home in the south, coming to a new valley . . .

She turned toward her bedside table for a pen. There were two envelopes leaning against the lamp, both addressed in Barney's handwriting.

TWENTY-ONE

A Paradise for Seabirds

THE LETTERS BOTH had London postmarks and had been sent on Friday. The first consisted of a hand-drawn picture of an island, with lots and lots of fairly basic birds, and five words: *Meet me at the castle.* There was a number too, written in Roman numerals — a date, ten days away.

The second letter was even shorter, and said only: *Bring package. Tell no one.*

Everything changed in an instant.

Barney had written!

He wanted to see her!

And before you cry, *Oh, Alice!* and *What?,* before you try to remind her about white nights and the hare story and the midnight picnics, and the unanswered emails and the not-turning-up-on-Visitors'-Day, and her promise to the major, and his face-your-fears speech — ask yourself what you would do if the person you loved most in the world asked you to meet him at a castle.

You might, of course, say, *No way! You let me down. Don't come creeping up to me with postcards and secrets and nonsensical ideas.*

Or you might give him another chance.

Alice loved Barney. It was as simple as that. She knew he wasn't perfect—she wasn't stupid. She knew, in her heart, that he was not a great actor, and she knew that there was something not quite right about his going away so much. But she thought —she hoped—that if she just believed in him enough, he would become who she wanted him to be.

I'm not saying that you would do what she did, or even that you should—but you might. If, in your deep heart's core, another chance was what you longed for.

And Alice did long. She longed very much indeed.

Alice did not think, as you might, that what Barney was asking was strange. This was, after all, the man who had once woken her in a blizzard in the middle of the night to make snow angels in the garden. And who one bright sunny day had turned up at school and faked a hospital appointment for her just so that they could drive to the beach. And who one year had organized an Easter egg hunt in the countryside around Cherry Grange so vast and so complicated that they were out climbing trees and scrabbling under hedges long after sunset, looking for chocolate.

Barney Mistlethwaite was quite the one for extravagant gestures.

The first thing was to work out what on earth he meant. Alice stared at the picture. There was an island, and there were birds . . . She closed her eyes and tried to think: Barney on her bed for a good-night cuddle . . . the mock sword fight with his phone . . .

Pow! Zap! Take that, vile intruder! What else had he written?

The Isle of . . . something . . . *is a paradise for ornithologists and seabirds* . . .

Yes—but the Isle of what?

She left the infirmary as soon as Matron let her and, without even bothering to change, went straight to the library. The rain had cleared up completely now, and the sky was a soft pale gray, almost white, with the loch a still sheet of silver. Most of the lower years were outside. The only people in the library were older students with exams coming up, who barely looked up as she passed. The air smelled of ink and paper and beeswax, and there were books from floor to ceiling. Usually, she found it impossible not to take one out to read. Today, however, she was on a different mission.

She found a free computer and typed in her search:

Scottish islands.

The first result informed her unhelpfully that there were more than 790 islands off the coasts of Scotland.

Scottish paradise for birds returned an avalanche of information about tropical plants.

Scottish seabirds . . . That was better! There was the arctic skua . . . the guillemot . . . the gannet . . . None of these rang any bells. The arctic tern . . . the great skua . . . the puffin!

Barney had definitely mentioned puffins.

Where are the Scottish puffins? she typed, and snorted with laughter at the comical picture of a small black and white bird with a huge striped beak, its head tilted curiously to the side. She stopped laughing when she realized that the puffins were everywhere, in far-flung places she had never heard of: Shetland, Noss, Muckle Flugga, Hermaness, Nish . . .

Nish! That was it! She was almost certain. She clicked to find out more.

The Isle of Nish is the largest of an archipelago of small islands and skerries lying west of Lumm, in Scotland, and part of the Inner Hebrides . . . Its area measures 59 square hectares, and its highest point is 103 meters . . .

Alice opened a map, but it gave no information other than a vague indication that the Isle of Nish lay off the western coast of

Scotland. She went on to Google Maps instead, typed in *Castle-haig*, then *Isle of Nish,* and clicked on *Directions.*

Aha!

School was a lot closer to the sea than she had imagined. One hour and twenty minutes driving, to be precise—longer walking, obviously . . . The thick blue line stopped by the sea, where you had to take a boat to Lumm, which you had to cross (two hours driving, about a million years walking) to catch another, smaller boat . . . All the boats' timetables varied hugely depending on the tides. She copied them down carefully, then peered more closely at the map itself. What a strange shape Scotland was—like a craggy giant's head, all lowering brows and hooked nose and chin, with deep scars where sea ran in. And no towns, not between here and the sea, barely even a road.

How was she supposed to get there?

TWENTY-TWO

Partners

FERGUS WAS CROSS. While Alice was in the library research-
ing seabird paradises, Fergus was mucking out the pigs.

The pigs were not the reason he was cross. Just as Alice now
enjoyed reveille, Fergus had grown fond of the pigs. Shoveling
poop and straw was hard, smelly work, but the pigs themselves
were reliable. The pigs came sniffing whenever he called them,
and they were always pleased to see him. The pigs were reliable,
which meant they didn't do things like run off on their own to
leap into boats and nearly drown. Fergus had seen Alice when
they carried her back to school, all white and wet and floppy, and
he had been terrified. They had pushed past him and all the other
curious students and teachers and taken her up to the infirmary,
and he had gone to the boathouse, where he had found the crate
of fireworks in the bottom of a boat, and taken one and wrapped

it carefully in plastic before placing it in his pocket, thinking she would like him to let it off over her grave as a tribute . . .

Then, when he realized his best friend was not dead at all, he was furious.

Yes, his best friend. He'd never told her, but that is how he thought of her. Though now you could make that his so-called best friend.

Or his ex–best friend.

Best friends, like fellow criminals, were proper partners. He'd never actually had a best friend before, but he was almost sure that was true. And proper partners didn't go haring off on their own to produce spectacular fireworks displays in the middle of lochs. Proper partners, he thought, shoveling pig-pee-soaked straw into a wheelbarrow, planned together.

Everything.

He was almost sure.

"Fergus!"

It was her—here—now! Well, he wouldn't speak to her. She'd see how it felt to be left out . . .

"Fergus!"

"WHAT?"

She was standing on the middle rung of the gate, dressed in pajamas tucked into wellies, under orange school waterproofs, her unbraided hair exploding down her back in wild curls under an orange school beanie.

She looked bonkers. His heart warmed.

"That was a mad, mad, mad thing to do," he growled.

"I know. I know! I'm sorry! But, Fergus, Fergus—do you want to do something even madder?"

A week later, the Great Orienteering Challenge began.

TWENTY-THREE

The Great
Orienteering Challenge

PICTURE A CASTLE, in a valley. A school bus driving out
through a pair of rusty gates.

There are thirty seventh-years inside the bus, and thirty
rucksacks full of sleeping bags and tents and provisions for three
days of camping. Soon, the students will be given their itinerar-
ies for the Great Orienteering Challenge. None of them know
where they will be going, except for Alice and Fergus, because
Fergus recently hacked into Madoc's computer and "rearranged"
his files.

He and Alice and Jesse are about to be given the itinerary
that will bring them closest to Barney Mistlethwaite's island.

This is Alice and Fergus's plan: Today, they will follow the
school's itinerary, which will take them toward the ferry for
Lumm. But tomorrow, they will follow their own path and head
for the Isle of Nish. The timing is tight, if they are to meet Barney

at the appointed date and be back for the Orienteering Challenge finish, but they have it all worked out. They will camp on the school-designated beach tonight, and on Lumm tomorrow. The next day, they will take the first boat to Nish, see Barney, take the last boat back, cross Lumm, catch another ferry to the mainland, camp, and the day after that hike to the finishing point without school being any the wiser.

What could possibly go wrong?

Don't worry too much about the details (Alice and Fergus certainly haven't). The plan is actually pretty much impossible, but Alice has convinced herself that it can be done, just as she convinced herself on receiving Barney's letter that it's a perfectly normal thing to be doing. Fergus is less convinced. Alice has fed him the vaguest of stories — that she's to meet Barney at the castle where he used to play as a child, that he's always wanted to show her his island paradise, that there are puffins she's wanted to see since she was tiny. He doesn't believe her, but he's going along for the ride, because he loves Alice and knows this means a lot to her, and because he also knows what it means to have useless parents and wants to be there for her if — when? — Barney doesn't turn up.

Both of them are trying not think what the Consequences would be of getting caught.

What else do you need to know?

They haven't told Jesse yet. They think there's more chance of convincing him once they're on the road. They're waiting to find the right moment to break it to him that he probably isn't going to win the Great Orienteering Challenge.

I told you, didn't I, that there would be at least two betrayals? This one is the second.

You want to know where Barney is? Right now, he's crisscrossing the North of England on a bus, on the run from some very nasty people. He's wearing a hat and sunglasses, and he's growing a beard.

Oh, and Alice has his parcel. Fergus doesn't know about that. She still hasn't opened it, but it's sitting at the bottom of her rucksack like a ticking bomb.

Madoc stopped the bus in the lay-by at the bottom of the hill.

"Are we there already, sir?" Duffy, as usual, hadn't been listening in class.

"No, we are not." Madoc reached into the glove compartment for a cardboard document wallet, pulled out a clutch of envelopes, and got up to distribute them around the bus. "Right, listen up, Year Seven! Each of these envelopes contains your itinerary, a map, a set of coordinates and instructions, the school's telephone number in case of emergencies, the emergency services telephone numbers, and also some emergency money."

"That's a lot of emergencies, sir," worried Samira. Madoc, who had severe misgivings about the Orienteering Challenge's potential to go wrong, replied that he would be staying at the youth hostel at Grigaich, right at the center of activities, and that the hostel's telephone number was also included in the pack.

An excited murmur followed him down the bus as groups began to discover where they were going. "What do these squiggly bits mean?" Zeb asked, and "Sir, which way is west?" cried Esme, and Amir questioned, "Is this blue line a road or a river?"

Jesse listened, feeling smug, his classmates' absurd questions further proof, if proof were needed, that most of them were clueless.

"We're going to the sea!" He beamed as he opened his group's itinerary. Immediately he spread out the map, his mind racing to plot out their route.

Alice and Fergus exchanged what was to be the first of many guilty looks.

"We might see otters . . . seals . . . dolphins!" cried Jesse. "This is going to be awesome!"

Madoc, back at the front of the bus, felt it would be a good idea to repeat the instructions Year Seven had heard so many times before yet seemed so intent on forgetting.

"Each set of coordinates relates to a campsite," he said. "Each team will be dropped off in a different location, and you will all be camping in a different place for each of your three nights, but you all have the same finishing point. The aim of the Challenge is for you to find your way to the three campsites and from there to the finishing point. The first group to arrive wins. Is that clear?"

"What happens if one of us breaks a leg, sir?" asked Jenny. "Or if we get lost, or ill, or fall down a crevasse?"

"None of those things is going to happen."

Madoc started the engine. Jesse grinned across the aisle at Alice and Fergus.

"We have so got this in the bag!" he whispered.

They both smiled tightly back.

TWENTY-FOUR

Someone Has to
Be in Charge

THE FEELING OF guilt worsened steadily as Alice and Fergus failed to find the right moment to tell Jesse the truth.

Jesse took control as soon as they were alone. Madoc had left them on the edge of a wide, grassy track stretching out over open moorland. The sun was shining, the breeze was light, the ground was soft but firm.

"Perfect conditions," Jesse declared. "Come along, team!"

Away he marched in long, easy strides, map in hand and compass at the ready. The other two stared uncomfortably at his retreating back.

They did not feel like a team.

"Should we tell him now?" asked Fergus.

"Oh, definitely," said Alice.

"Are you coming or what?" Jesse, already a hundred meters ahead, tapped his watch.

"We'll tell him later," said Fergus as they hurried after him.

"When he's not in such a hurry," agreed Alice.

But Jesse hurried relentlessly throughout the morning.

He read the map. He followed the compass. He ran ahead to check landmarks, then back to Alice and Fergus to encourage them on. He made them sing a marching song. When they had to climb over a recent rockfall, he showed them how to look for holds in the rock, and shimmied up before them to help.

"Don't look down," he warned.

"It's not that high," Alice said, then did look down and was very glad to take his hand.

When they stopped by a stream to eat, they discovered that Jesse had already organized their lunch into Tupperware boxes. And when Fergus, parched, tried to drink from the stream, Jesse pushed his hand away before it even reached his mouth, saying, "Don't! You have to purify it first. You never know what might have died upstream. You could get really ill."

Setting out that morning, Fergus had been excited about the Orienteering Challenge. He wondered now if perhaps what had excited him had been the thrill of plotting with Alice. He certainly hadn't reckoned on corpses, or on Jesse being so overbearing.

"Died?" he asked. "Like what?"

"You know. A rat! A sheep! A cow! Anything!"

"Well, aren't you the fount of all knowledge," Fergus grumbled.

"I just love it, I guess." Jesse chose to ignore the jibe, and gazed around their picnic spot. "Isn't this amazing?"

And when someone is so happy, and helpful, and knowledgeable, how do you ask them to do something that goes completely against everything they want? Alice, who had been about to speak, took another bite of sandwich. Fergus batted away a mosquito, risen from the potentially corpse-infected water.

They said nothing. But the longer they left it, the harder it got.

That is usually the way, with betrayal.

Poor Jesse! For all his appearance of enjoyment, he too was finding the day difficult.

They say that in a group of three, one person always feels left out. In Jesse's experience, that person was always him. He already knew that Alice and Fergus had a special friendship. He just wished that on this trip, they wouldn't make it so obvious. He had noticed some of the looks they had exchanged that morning when they thought he wasn't looking. Always one to feel hard done by, he imagined they were laughing at him for taking the Challenge so seriously. But just as in a trio there is always one who feels left out, so in a group someone has to be in charge, and in this particular group he believed—somewhat unfairly—that everything depended on him. Alice and Fergus were hopeless map readers, he told himself. They didn't even know how to put up the tent! When they'd practiced at school, Jesse had had to do everything! And when he thought back to the orienteering exercise, when they had both run straight into a bog, he wasn't sure they even realized how badly that could have ended if he hadn't been there.

And on top of all that, Fergus had tried to drink the stream water! No, if they stood a chance of surviving—let alone winning—Jesse was convinced that he, and he alone, must be in charge. Which was fine by him. He knew the other two didn't really care about winning, but he was confident that as long as they did exactly what they were told, everything would be fine.

Probably.

He just hadn't anticipated how heavy responsibility would feel.

They set off after lunch on a narrow sheep track along the stream, which almost immediately disappeared, forcing them to clamber from rock to rock and bank to bank to maintain a steady reading on the compass. Alice, lost in thoughts of Barney and the days to come, fell in the water, and they had to stop for her to change her socks.

"Are you sure this is right?" Fergus asked.

"We have to follow the stream."

"Only, my socks are getting wet too."

Jesse, who longed to enjoy the walk, told himself this was going to be a very long three days, and got out his binoculars.

"There's a bridge," he announced. "Exactly what I was looking for. Our road goes over it."

Even Alice, who had absolute faith in Jesse, was disappointed by the so-called road, which looked like it had not been used for decades, with most of the tarmac eroded and long grass growing in the middle.

"It is the right road." Jesse shoved the map at the others. Alice, sensing his irritation, stared at it politely. Fergus yawned. "This is the bridge, and this is the stream, and this is where we are now. So we walk along here for about two hundred meters—Come on, walk!" They jumped, and followed as he set off with his nose in the map. "And there's a hump in the road, and we go over the hill, and we come to a gate, and we go through that and there's a path into these woods and . . . Ah."

In his life, Jesse had never felt so mortified.

Which, in a way, turned out to be a good thing, because the other two noticed, and were sorry.

TWENTY-FIVE

Somewhere a Lark

THEY HAD INDEED come to a gate, and there was indeed a path, and there were woods, but there was also a big wooden sign saying KEEP OUT in big red letters, with another sign underneath in only slightly smaller letters saying CONTROL YOUR DOG OR WE WILL SHOOT IT. On the other side of the gate, a herd of deer were grazing in a field surrounded by an electric fence.

"Doesn't it show private property on the map?" asked Fergus.

"It's meant to be a public footpath." Jesse could have cried with the unfairness of it. "Sometimes landowners don't respect the rules. We'll just have to go around the field."

But the field stretched on forever.

"Or we could just go over the gate," suggested Alice. "Like we're meant to."

"The sign says Keep Out!"

"We don't have a dog," said Fergus.

"No, but they have guns." Jesse sighed. "It has to be the field. Look, there's a path. Sort of. Let's go."

Faced with their first real setback, the dynamics between the children shifted. Jesse, forced to accept he was not invincible, realized that the other two were not quite as hopeless as he had thought. Fergus, seeing Jesse's genuine distress about the closed footpath, became less peevish. Alice stopped daydreaming and focused on the task at hand.

They set off, Jesse first, then Alice, then Fergus. They did not complain, not even when the sort-of path turned out not to be a path at all but a sheep track even worse than the one by the stream. When their shoulders brushed the overgrown ferns that edged it, releasing clouds of midges, which got into their hair and clothes and up their noses, they just pulled their jackets close and their hoods up. The sun beat down and they roasted and the midges got in anyway, but they never so much as squeaked.

Roots tripped them. Brambles tore at their hands and clothes. Jesse, looking at the compass, walked into a tree and cut his temple. Fergus was devoured by the intrusive midges, and Alice got a rash where her rucksack rubbed her shoulders. But when, twenty minutes later, the fern forest spat them out into the open —bloody, puffy, and raw—they felt like a team.

For now.

"The good news," Jesse said, "is that after this, it should be open country."

"And the bad news?"

"We've walked about three miles in the wrong direction."

"So what do we do next?"

Jesse held out the compass. "We go that way, to the sea."

Empty moorland, crisscrossed by streams and dotted with clumps of heather, stretched before them toward a horizon of hills.

"Are you sure?" Fergus asked.

"Fergus!" Alice scolded, holding back a smile. "The compass never lies!"

They passed a stream and filled their water bottles, and while they waited for their purifying tablets to dissolve, they soaked T-shirts in the current and wrapped them round their heads to cool down.

"We look like the three kings," said Fergus. "You know, from Christmas? They crossed mountains and deserts with gifts."

"Two kings," corrected Alice. "One queen."

Jesse took a swig of chlorinated water.

"If I had a gift," he said, "it would be lemonade, made with real lemons the way my dad does in the summer."

"If I had a gift," said Alice, sniffing delicately at her shirt, "it would be a bath."

"If I had a gift," said Fergus, yawning, "it would be a bed."

And they lay side by side and looked at the sky, and thought how lovely it was.

Then up they got and on they trudged, across the plain and up a first hill and then a second and a third, bending under the weight of their rucksacks. Their heels and toes blistered, their muscles ached, and their stomachs rumbled. It seemed quite impossible that this morning had begun at school, and that tomorrow would take them somewhere else again. They walked in a trance, in which only now existed, up and up, one foot in front of the other until—finally—they reached the top, and a path that Jesse said was the one they were meant to be on all along, and . . . Oh!

Sometimes the beauty of the world . . .

The major was right. It could leave you breathless.

The landscape on this side of the hill was different again. The ground falling away beneath them was lush and green, dotted with copses of trees and clumps of blazing yellow gorse. Flowers grew in the grass, golden buttercups and purple thistles, wild hyacinths and wispy cotton grass. Rabbits scattered before them as they walked, white tails bobbing.

Somewhere, a lark was singing.

"Look!" said Fergus.

Far below, a white crescent of beach. On the horizon, purple islands rising out of the mists. And as far as they could see, beyond the beach and the islands, blue, blue, blue.

They had found the sea.

It took them another hour to reach the beach, but walking felt easy now that they could see where they were going. The light on the water, playing tricks, turned the sea gold as they came down the hill. The beach — not sand, but tiny crushed shells — sparkled. As they reached sea level, they passed a brook, falling the last few meters in a rainbow waterfall where sparrows bathed. They saw a copse of trees and, tucked among them, an old fisherman's hut with no door and only half a roof.

"Yes!" Jesse fist-pumped the air. "Exactly what it says on the itinerary! Who's the best map reader EVER? WHO? WHO?"

He strode into the cottage through the space where the door would have been, and out again into a walled patch of grass that had once been the garden.

"This will be a perfect camping spot. Right, team! Let's pitch the tent! Who wants to dig a fire pit? We need water for . . . Guys?"

The others had not followed him into the garden.

"Alice? Fergus?"

Nothing. Jesse felt a sudden, unreasonable fear that they had left him.

"Guys?"

"We're here!"

His jaw dropped as Alice ran out of the cottage in a swimsuit, followed by Fergus in a startling pair of royal-blue polka-dotted boxer shorts.

The swimsuit, by the way, should have been a clue—why would Alice have packed one, if she didn't know she was going to be near a beach? But Jesse didn't think about that till later. For now, he was too busy panicking.

"Come swimming!" Alice cried.

"Swimming?" They were mad, Jesse thought. They would die, or at least get hypothermia! And they were hours from anywhere!

"Come on!" Alice insisted. "We'll wait, but hurry because I'm getting cold!"

"But it'll be even colder in the water!"

"STOP BEING SUCH A FUSSYPANTS, JESSE, AND GET YOUR CLOTHES OFF!" yelled Fergus.

They pounced, a two-pronged attack, ignoring his cries of protest. They grabbed his hands and dragged him toward the shore, and when he saw they weren't going to give in, he gave up and ran toward the water with them, shedding his clothes along the beach as he went.

All together, they ran into the sea. Jesse screamed as the cold hit him. Fergus almost immediately turned blue.

"It's like ice made of diamonds," Alice shouted. "I'm going under."

She dived into a wave, and then of course they had to do the same. The cold stole their breath and clamped their brains. Every pore of their skin tingled; every hair on their heads stood on end. Afterwards, to warm up, they chased each other through the shallows, kicking up water and shouting, with no one to hear them but the gulls, and there was no place for plots and Challenges, only laughter.

The beauty of the world will do that for you.

TWENTY-SIX

The North Star

ALICE LOVED IT HERE, she loved it. But the major could have told her that just as fear is a part of courage, so loss is a part of love. Alice knew only that she had set out from school thinking of the old life that lay ahead, but now that she was gone all she could think about was the new life she had left behind. And despite the euphoria of finishing the walk and the wild joy of the swim, she felt suddenly and unaccountably afraid.

Once they were dry, with warm fleeces pulled over salt-tight skin, Fergus — feeling guilty about what was to come — insisted that he and Alice would put up the tent, leaving Jesse free to fish off the rocks at the end of the beach.

"No," Jesse said. "No, no, no, no, no."

"We are honestly not as useless as you think," Fergus said. "Go and fish! Enjoy yourself!"

Jesse, feeling very daring, went fishing.

The bendy poles that held up the tent did not bend in quite the way Fergus thought they should, and there was a bad moment when Alice realized she had forgotten to pack the tent pegs, but with a little prodding and coaxing and improvising with sticks, the tent went up — a little flappier than it should have been and not quite straight, but definitely up.

"Hurrah!" Fergus was delighted. "I said we could do it! Oh, and look — Jesse's caught a fish!"

At the end of the beach, Jesse, quite wild with excitement, was performing a sort of victory dance in his boxer shorts and orange waterproof jacket, waving a large silver fish. Fergus waved energetically back.

"Wave, Alice! Poor guy, even I feel sorry for him, having to deal with us all day. Alice! Why aren't you waving?"

Alice, lost in thought, was gazing across the sea at the islands. She started as he prodded her in the ribs. "Sorry, what?"

"Jesse! He caught a fish! Wave! You're miles away!"

"I was just . . . Fergus, are we mad?"

"To be running off to find your dad?" he asked cheerfully. "We're more than mad, we're insane! Plus, it's really unfair to Jesse."

"Be serious!"

They were walking along the beach now, above the high-tide

mark. Fergus reached down to pick up a piece of driftwood and considered his answer.

"Where do you suppose this came from?" he asked.

"I don't know! America? Fergus!"

"Or Greenland?" he said. "Or Norway, or Sweden? Or Russia! I think, tonight, we should make the biggest bonfire any of us has ever seen, and burn it."

"Fergus, what are you going on about?"

"I don't know, to be honest. Nonsense, probably. I suppose I just mean we're here now, so let's enjoy it."

And they did.

They cooked Jesse's fish over a small fire and agreed that, even with all the sand they ate with it, it was the best meal they'd ever had. Three seals swam into the bay as they were eating, three sleek black heads bobbing in the quiet waves just offshore, with silvery whiskers and bright, curious eyes. They put on a show as the three humans watched, diving and bobbing back up, turning lazily in the water, then disappeared as suddenly as they'd come, into waves turned indigo and gold by the endlessly setting summer sun. The children ran down to the water to look for the seals. The seals did not return, but Jesse swore that he had seen a flipper, waving.

When they were sure the seals were gone, they gathered armfuls of driftwood and built the cooking fire into Fergus's giant bonfire, which burned in a great blaze on the sand, the salt on the wood catching in a shower of blue sparks.

"Do you know what the French word for *bonfire* is?" Fergus asked.

"What?" asked Jesse.

"Feu de joie," said Fergus. "It means 'fire of joy.'"

"Fire of joy," said Jesse. "I like that."

Across the sea, the evening mist was rising, shrouding the bruised islands. The air grew cold, even by the fire. Stars came out. Jesse pointed at the brightest one.

"The North Star," he said. "The one sailors use to find their way home."

Home. Alice felt a pang as she thought of the major, his hand on her head like a blessing. *This is your home,* he had said. What would he say if he found out about their plan? Suddenly, it felt impossible that he would not. She made herself think of Barney instead. She tried to picture herself running toward him across a beach like this one, throwing herself into his arms so that he could swing her high into the air the way he always used to do when she was little. He was probably by some quay right now, getting into a boat, sailing, surrounded by seals, across a star-strewn sea toward the purple islands to wait for her. But for once, her imagination failed her.

The problem was, she wasn't little anymore.

In that moment, she wanted more than anything to abandon her plans. But then she reminded herself of something else the major had said: *To be fearless, we must first banish our fears, and to achieve that, we must look them in the face.*

She was terrified—not of the trip itself, but of what she might find at the end. And she didn't know if she was being brave or reckless, but she knew she had to see this through.

"That swim! And those stars! The bonfire! The fish—the seals!" The ceiling of the flappy, pegless tent lurched dramatically over where Jesse lay on his back, staring straight at it, but he was too drunk with the day's events to even notice. "Guys, this is awesome!"

"Long day tomorrow, Jesse," said Fergus, with a sidelong glance at Alice. "Try to get some sleep."

"I can't," Jesse confessed. "It feels like my head's exploding. I mean, I knew orienteering was going to be great, but this is amazing."

"It's not the orienteering that's amazing, it's the beach." Fergus yawned. "Orienteering's just a load of maps."

"Just a load of maps?" Jesse flipped onto his side and stared at Fergus, astounded. "Just a load of maps? Maps are like . . ." He searched carefully for the right words. "Maps are what make the world fit together. You can go anywhere you want if you have a map. Which means . . ."

He paused, astounded by a sudden realization.

"What?" asked Fergus.

"Which means that maybe," Jesse said carefully, "if you can go anywhere you want, you can be anything you want as well."

Alice, who had been listening in silence, asked, "What do you want to be?"

"Not a violinist," said Jesse.

"Well, no," Fergus agreed.

Alice frowned, then raised her eyebrows, as if to ask, *What about you, then?*

"Oh, I'll be a genius," Fergus said. "I just need to decide what sort."

"I'll be a writer." Even as she said it, Alice knew that just saying *a writer* wasn't enough. It was beginning to dawn on her that there are as many different sorts of writers as there are different sorts of stories. Sooner or later, she was going to have to choose which stories she wanted to tell, and how.

"Jesse?" asked Fergus. "You haven't said."

"I don't know! Something outside."

"You should be an explorer," Alice said quietly. "You've got a real talent for it."

Fergus laughed. "Spoken like a true Locker."

An explorer! The more Jesse thought about it, the more he liked it.

"All right," he said. "I will."

Lost in thoughts of their brilliant futures, they fell asleep, lulled by the song of the sea, while farther north, on a shadowy quay, Barney Mistlethwaite looked around for a boat to steal.

TWENTY-SEVEN

The Great Explorer

I F YOU ARE planning to ask someone to do something as a favor to you that they really don't want to do, you'd best have a convincing argument ready. And if you are embarking on a highly illicit expedition, you'd do well to have a clear idea of the strengths and weaknesses of your plan. It will help when you encounter those inevitable obstacles.

Jesse and his orienteering skills were the great strength of Alice and Fergus's plan. His absolute determination to win the Orienteering Challenge and his well-known strict adherence to school rules were its fatal weaknesses.

On the morning of their second day, Jesse emerged from a long, deep sleep in excellent spirits, which were lifted even further when he discovered that Alice and Fergus had risen before him, that they had made tea and porridge, and that the porridge was actually good. Even the weather, which had turned cold and gray overnight, could not dampen his mood.

"Not such a long walk today," he said, shoveling down his breakfast. "Two hours south along the coast, I reckon, then three hours inland, but all on tracks and roads. Add in a stop for lunch, and a couple of rests, that's six hours, plus we've got to pack up here and the weather's not . . . What? Why are you looking at me like that?"

"Tell him," said Fergus.

And so the second betrayal began.

Alice fed Jesse the same unconvincing lies she had told Fergus —Barney and the castle where she was to meet him, the island paradise he longed to show her, the puffins . . . Jesse's reaction went from bafflement—"Island? Castle? Puffins? What are you talking about?"—to hurt—"You've known all this time and didn't tell me?"—to flat refusal—"I'm not going, and I'll tell school."

"Please, Jesse," said Alice. "We need you."

"Need me?"

"You're the best orienteer. A great orienteer."

"Don't try and flatter me! How long have you been plotting this?"

"Not long," lied Alice.

"Ages," admitted Fergus.

"Why are you doing this?" demanded Jesse.

"I do wonder, sometimes," said Fergus. "But it's important to Alice."

"Will you do it?" Alice asked.

An uncomfortable lump was forming in Jesse's throat. That they had plotted this for ages! That they had known, yesterday on the beach, and last night by the fire, and before going to sleep in the tent! Known, and kept it from him, and made a fool of him! *You should be an explorer*—that he should have felt so happy, when they were about to stab him in the back, knowing how much this Challenge meant to him, knowing how much their friendship . . .

"No," he said. "I won't."

Fergus, who really was wondering about the plan, whooped silently, then sighed as Alice set her chin in a way he was beginning to recognize.

"Then we'll just have to do it without you," she said in a very small voice.

"Alice!" he whispered. "We can't! Not without Jesse!"

"I'll go alone if I have to."

He tried to reason with her. "Think of the Consequences if Jesse gets back without us! School will know we split up—he'll have to tell them!"

"I know. I'm sorry."

Despite the chin, there was an unmistakable quaver in her voice. And Fergus knew that he could never let her go alone.

Silently, they washed their bowls, packed up their rucksacks, and dismantled the tent.

"You should take it," Alice told Jesse. "It's only fair." She hesitated, then, standing on tiptoe, kissed him quickly on the cheek. "Good luck, Jesse. I'm sure you'll win."

"Please come with us, Jesse." Fergus couldn't believe this was happening. Now that they were separating, he realized how much it meant to him for them to all be together. Not because they might—would probably—get lost without Jesse, but because, astonishingly, he liked him.

And oh, thought Jesse, the swim and the stars and the bonfire and the fish! The seals, and the sound of the waves at night!

"I'm not coming," he said. "And that's that."

"Alice!" begged Fergus. "Let's talk about this!"

But Alice was already walking, and Jesse was looking away. Fergus sighed, swung his pack onto his back, and ran after her.

The beach was pristine again, all traces of their fire wiped clean by the tide. Jesse thought he saw a sleek black head in the water, but it was only driftwood, bobbing.

"I'm going to win this," he said out loud. "I'll show them!"

His words scattered on the wind.

Alice and Fergus were nearing an intersection on the path

they had come down the day before. Jesse knew, without even looking at the map, that if they wanted to go north, they had to turn left. Whereas he had to go right. Right, and then inland, and then he would win, because no one was faster or better than him. Especially with no one to slow him down. He would win.

He would win!

Except—could he even win if he lost half his team?

His heart tightened. He had loved being part of their team. They had stopped now and were looking at the map.

"Left," Jesse muttered. "It's not difficult. LEFT!" They turned right. He waved. They didn't see. He shouted. They didn't hear. "Oh, come on," he groaned. It was true—they couldn't do it without him.

That wasn't surprising. What was surprising was that he didn't want them to. "WAIT!" he shouted again, and this time they looked back, and stopped, and grinned. "Wait for me!" he bellowed, and began to run. After all, Jesse had always longed for a real adventure. Here it was, just begging him to join in.

TWENTY-EIGHT

The Mosquito Woman

O F COURSE, there is still the question of the parcel at the bottom of Alice's rucksack, which will shortly be making its full and dramatic entry into this story.

Pictures of the contents of that parcel have been splashed all over the internet, and all over newspapers all over the world. A lot of people want those contents: The police. Private detectives. Some dangerous criminals. Barney Mistlethwaite.

He's the only one who knows Alice has it.

But—as you know—people are after him.

Which means they're getting closer to her.

Jesse didn't explain his change of heart, and Alice and Fergus didn't ask, but none of them had stopped grinning since he'd joined them.

"I reckon I've saved two hours from the route you'd planned," he informed them when they stopped for a meager lunch of tuna and oatcakes. "Even if you had been going in the right direction. Which you weren't."

"Go on, rub it in." Fergus beamed. "Do not let an occasion pass without reminding us of your tremendous superiority."

"He *is* superior," Alice said affectionately. "He's a positive marvel."

"A marvel!" Jesse grunted to hide his smile, and went back to the map. "So we follow this path"—he traced a dotted line across the headland—"and we get to this village, where we catch the ferry that will take us to the town of Moraig, on Lumm."

"An actual town?" asked Fergus. "With cars and people and potentially shops where we can buy actual food?"

"We have actual food," Jesse said.

"I'm not sure we do," said Fergus. "We have oatcakes, and tuna. I don't believe those are food. Neither is porridge, for that matter. I don't think I've ever been so hungry in my life."

"There's a boat at two o'clock," said Alice. "Can we make it? We need to get across Lumm this afternoon so that we can catch the boat to Nish tomorrow morning. It's the only one, so we can't miss it."

"We can be at the ferry in an hour if we hurry," said Jesse.

"Then let's go! Fergus, you can eat while we walk!"

On they went over the undulating land, three friends, happy

and carefree and rebellious, jogging on the downhills, striding across the flat, skipping on the uphills, blisters and aching muscles forgotten. Fergus, whistling tunelessly, reflected on how criminal master plans were even better when three people were involved. Jesse, feeling a little dazed that he was here, heading north instead of south, was being a knight on a quest. And Alice surprised herself by thinking how much she loved them both.

As they came down again to sea level, the air grew damp and claggy with salt. Mist rose from dips and hollows, clung in beads to blades of grass, hugged the ground like a shroud. The road, when they came to it, was narrow and potholed. Houses began to appear, looming out of the whiteness like ghosts. They stamped their feet as they walked—for warmth, Jesse said, but also for the comfort of noise in a muffled world.

They almost missed the turn. The bashed-up, rusty sign for the ferry, white with the black outline of a boat, was half hidden behind a holly tree. Jesse and Alice walked straight past it, and Fergus saw it only by chance, because he stopped to tie a shoelace.

They turned down an even narrower road.

"I thought somehow it would be . . ." Alice screwed up her face as she tried to find the right word.

"Bigger?" suggested Fergus. "Less like a road to absolutely nowhere?"

There were no shops, or even houses. The quay appeared to just be the bit where the road went into the water.

"Before you ask," said Jesse, "this is definitely what the map says. Also, there was that sign."

Doubtfully, they considered the quay, put down their rucksacks, and sat, huddled together on the road, with their hoods pulled up against the cold.

"It's like the station at Castlehaig," Jesse said, trying to be positive. "You think no one's coming, but they do."

"That's true," said Alice firmly. "They do."

"They'll have just finished lunch at school," said Fergus. "It was shepherd's pie today. I looked at the menu before I left. I love shepherd's pie."

"There'll be shepherd's pie again," promised Alice. "When we get back. There's always shepherd's pie."

"If we get back," said Fergus darkly.

"Something's coming," Jesse said.

The boat loomed out of the mist like a monster, a flock of gulls swirling in its wake, and came to stop by the quay in a great churning of gray-brown water. A ramp came down. The three scrambled to their feet. A red-faced man in yellow oilskins signaled for them to stay back as a tractor lumbered off the ferry, followed by a small white car and a group of cyclists. The oilskin man waved them on.

"You lot escaped from a prison or something?" he asked, eyeing their orange jackets.

"Je ne comprends pas," said Fergus, in his best Madame Gilbert French. "Trois enfants, s'il vous plaît."

He held up three fingers, pointing to himself, Alice, and Jesse. The other two stared, astonished, as the oilskin man produced tickets.

"What did you do that for?" whispered Alice as they walked away.

"We're on the run," he whispered back. "We have to have a disguise! It doesn't work otherwise."

Laughing, they ran onto the passenger deck, where they lined up against a railing, facing the mainland. The sea was dark, sullen gray, with white crests blown back by a sharp wind. Farther out, a sailing yacht raced across the water, tilted at an impossible angle, and a cormorant was fishing. Lumm was only a few miles away—they could already see its dark mass ahead—but they felt like voyagers setting off on an uncharted journey, all the more exciting because no one in the world knew where they were.

The ferry blasted a horn, making them all jump. They waved goodbye to the mainland.

"Au revoir!" shouted Fergus, dizzy with linguistic success.

"Au revoir!" Alice repeated, while Jesse, feeling hilarious, shouted goodbye in English but with a mock French accent.

And here was danger now, very nearly upon them . . .

A red car was tearing down the road to the quay. It skidded to a halt by the water and two large men dressed in black spilled out, waving and shouting at the ferry. "Aspetti! Wait!"

"What's that?" asked Jesse.

"Not French," said Fergus. "I don't think."

"Italian?" said Alice. "Maybe?"

But the ramp was already up, the water churning again. The ferry didn't wait. The men dropped their arms in defeat, turned back toward the car, and stood by the near-side rear door, heads respectfully bowed. The car door opened and a tiny woman stepped out, dressed simply in black leggings and a thick black parka, with long hair tucked into a knitted black cap, and a pair of enormous mosquito sunglasses. In her flat-soled boots, she barely reached the men's shoulders, but there was no question who was in charge.

The mosquito woman raised her hand to the ferry and pointed.

Fergus laughed and waved, but Alice shivered.

She had the feeling the woman was pointing straight at her.

TWENTY-NINE

Oyster!

MORAIG WAS A pretty harbor, with houses all painted different colors tumbling down steep hills toward the water, and a parade of busy shops. Under blue skies, it would have been a cheerful scene. But the weather had worsened during the crossing. The sky had grown menacing with low, heavy clouds, and the air was pregnant with the anticipation of thunder. The shoppers had an urgency about them. No one dallied to browse or chat, but hurried home to prepare for the storm as soon as they had paid.

"I've been here before," Fergus said suddenly as they walked from the ferry into town. He stopped at the top of a steep flight of steps leading to a little beach. "I think I came with my parents! Can we go down?"

Jesse peered fretfully at the clouds. "If we miss this bus, we'll have to find somewhere to camp near here tonight. The next bus isn't for another two hours, and we really need to get the tent up before the storm."

"If we camp here, we'll miss tomorrow's boat to Nish. Also . . ." Alice glanced over her shoulder toward their ferry, which was already sailing back out of the harbor. Presumably, when it returned, it would be bringing the passengers left behind on the quayside, including the woman who had pointed at her. Alice had not shared her unease about the red-car people with Fergus and Jesse, and she couldn't have explained why, but she didn't want to be here when they arrived.

"We've got twenty minutes till the bus." Fergus gazed longingly at the sand. "And it stops right here by the steps."

"No way," said Jesse. "What if the bus comes early, and you're still on the beach, and it doesn't wait? You can go on our way back from—"

"It's fine," Alice interrupted softly. "Go. We'll shout if the bus comes."

"I'll be quick!" Fergus promised.

He scrambled down the steps and ran toward the water, then struck out along the sand toward the dark rocks at the far end of the beach.

"Why did you let him go?" complained Jesse. "It's not even like it's a nice beach. It smells of fish." He wrinkled his nose. "And not in a good way."

"He came with his parents," murmured Alice. "So it matters."

Jesse would have liked to ask her more about Fergus and his parents, and also about hers, but she had that faraway, dreamy look about her that he knew meant she wouldn't talk.

The wind picked up, and the sky darkened. Boats came into the harbor on waves swollen by the rising tide. When the bus came, the driver did not want to wait, and Fergus, who had lingered at the far end of the beach, ran until he was red in the face. As the bus wound its way through the hills and valleys of the island, he grew paler and paler. By the time they reached their destination, he was ghost white, and sweating.

The bus left them near the quay in a medium-sized village. Unlike the quay on the mainland, this one had a car park, a proper dock, a long low building marked TICKETS and INFORMATION, and a harbor full of boats, all anchored offshore in preparation for the coming storm. Alice would have liked to linger, to ask which was the boat to Nish and whether she could see the island from here, but Jesse wouldn't let her. The wind was blowing hard now, the air was damp with the promise of rain, and they still had a way to go before they could pitch their tent at the campsite Jesse had found on the map.

"We have to pitch the tent before the storm," Jesse repeated, and led the others back along the road the bus had come in on, turning left a hundred meters after the village onto a narrow tree-lined track with open marshland on either side. After five hundred meters, they passed a solitary white stone house, set back from the track in an overgrown garden. Two hundred meters after that, they arrived at the campsite, which was small, empty, and basic, with just a trash can, a water tap, and a locked toilet, and only partly sheltered from the wind by a bank of trees and a stone wall. Beyond the campsite, hidden from view by the trees, was the sea, roaring with angry waves.

"Let's get to work." Jesse shrugged off his rucksack and began to pull out the tent.

Fergus wrapped his arms around himself and said, "I'm going to the beach."

"Again?" Jesse was outraged. "Fergus, the tent! The rain! We have to be ready! Fergus!"

"Leave him." Alice laid a hand on Jesse's arm as Fergus left.

"But it's not fair!"

"We'll manage."

Jesse, grumbling, let it go.

A squalling wind played havoc with their work. The canvas flapped wildly as they opened the tent, then refused to be stilled. By the time they had finished, there was not a straight edge or right angle to the tent.

"We need Fergus back now, before the rain starts," said Jesse, looking at the sky. "Or it'll be wet in there as well as wonky."

"I'll go and get him," said Alice.

It was a smaller beach than the last one, a white cove almost completely submerged by battering waves. Alice pulled her hood up against the wind, and battled her way along the narrow sand to where Fergus sat just above the high-tide line, facing the water.

"Come back!" she shouted as she approached. "Jesse says we have to get inside before it rains!"

"I like it here!" he shouted back.

Alice flopped down beside him on the ground.

"Jesse really will go mad," she said.

"I don't care."

In the weeks she had known him, Alice had never seen Fergus so dejected. She leaned back on her elbows and raised inquiring eyebrows.

"I was little," Fergus said at last. "Probably six or seven. We did a tour of the Scottish islands. I think we stopped in Moraig for one night. I don't really remember much, just that we were all together."

Alice squeezed his arm.

"You know what, Alice? I hope we don't make it back in time. I hope we get stuck on your dad's island, and school sends out a massive search party, just like I always wanted, and my parents almost die of worry. Parents are useless, Alice. They just are."

"Hmm," she said.

"I'm sorry." Fergus had gone very pale, and she worried that he might cry.

"It's fine, Fer. Really. But we do have to go now because it's going to rain soon. Come on. Come and help and have something to eat."

"I'm not hungry."

The rain started, a few fat drops, then stopped, as though the clouds were holding their breath. Alice stood up, pulling Fergus up after her. The line between the sea and the sky had disappeared. Both were the color of lead.

"I am not hungry," Fergus repeated. "Because I have eaten an oyster."

"An oyster!"

"It's something Mum and Dad used to do on holidays. Eat oysters straight off the rocks. I picked one on the beach in Moraig. Alice, I think I'm going to be—"

As the heavens opened, he threw up in the sand.

THIRTY

Darkly Lit Against the Sky

ALICE AND FERGUS were drenched in seconds. Alice, struggling against the howling wind, dragging a green-faced Fergus, tried not to gag when he was sick again and his vomit splattered her arm.

The trees around the campsite were bent almost horizontal in the wind. Jesse, in full waterproof gear, was staggering toward the tent with his arms full of stones to make up for the missing tent pegs.

"Where have you been?" he shouted at the others. "Help me!"

Fergus crumpled to his knees. Alice tried to pull him up. He moaned and curled up in a ball in the wet sand. Jesse dropped his stones and ran toward them.

"Get up!" Alice shouted at Fergus (she may have kicked him a little). "GET UP!"

"What happened?" cried Jesse.

"I think he's got food poisoning!"

"What? But he hasn't eaten anything!"

"Just help me, Jesse!"

Together, Alice and Jesse hauled Fergus off the ground, then turned toward the tent . . .

"Oh no," said Jesse. "Oh no, oh no, oh no . . ."

The tent was gone.

The weight of their three rucksacks had prevented it from flying very far. But a strong squall had inflated the fabric like a sail, dragged it across the campsite, and flung it in a sodden heap against the wall.

Jesse let go of Fergus and ran. Alice, after a moment's hesitation, went after him. Fergus, left alone, doubled over and retched.

"How bad is it?" shouted Alice.

"Bad!"

The tent was wedged into the wall, the guy ropes tangled around the rungs of the gate. Alice and Jesse tugged and pulled, picked at knots with frozen fingers. Part of the fabric had caught on a rusty rung. As Jesse struggled to wrestle it off, another squall slapped it across his face. Even in the gale, they heard the sound of fabric ripping.

They had to face the truth.

No one was ever going to sleep in it again.

They were alone, far from home, on an island, in a storm,

with water running down their necks, through their clothes, and into their boots. Nobody knew where they were, and they were scared.

For a few seconds, which felt much longer, nobody said anything. Then Fergus sneezed, and Jesse shook himself and hauled the rucksacks from the folds of the ruined tent.

"We'll have to go back to the village," Jesse said. "We'll ask for help at the pub."

It was the end, and they all knew it. No pub landlord would take in three lost, drenched children without asking questions. The adventure was over before it had really begun, the Challenge was lost, Barney would not be met on his island. Of the three, Alice felt the regret the keenest, but all their hearts were breaking.

Wearily, silently, the runaways turned back along the road. Jesse shouldered his own rucksack and Fergus's. Alice carried hers. Between them, they supported Fergus. They stopped at the entrance of the campsite to put the tent in the trash. It wouldn't fit. Jesse swore.

"Just leave it," said Alice.

"And have it blow into the sea and get eaten by some poor whale, or strangle a dolphin?" asked Jesse savagely. "I don't think so."

A jag of lightning tore open the sky. A rumble of thunder

responded. There was a shriek, and a terrible splintering sound. A shadow rushed toward them.

A hundred meters ahead, a tree thumped across the road, exactly where they would have been if they had not stopped.

For a few moments, again, nobody said a word. Then, shaking, Jesse said, "We'll have to walk around it."

"No!" Alice put out a hand to hold him back. "The rain! Remember when we got stuck on the orienteering exercise? Look at the ground! The track's almost a river. Those are marshes around us, Jesse, we'll sink!"

"WELL, WHAT, THEN?" Jesse yelled.

Another flash of lightning. For a few seconds, the silhouette of the house they had passed earlier appeared, darkly lit against the sky.

"There!" Alice shouted, and half ran, half stumbled toward it.

THIRTY-ONE

Mega-Super-Fun

*C*ALVA. THAT WAS the name of the house, painted in white on a black sign nailed to the wooden gate. The three staggered up a short unpaved drive to a small porch and hammered on the front door.

Nobody came.

"What now?" asked Alice.

"Let's look round the back," said Jesse.

Still supporting Fergus, they walked through a tangled garden to a lawn overlooked by large sash windows.

"HELLO? HELLO?"

The rain fell harder. Still nobody came.

"No locks," said Jesse, pressing his face to one of the windows. "And the catch looks old. Stand back."

The others watched, astonished, as he seized the handles of the upper sash and yanked it downward. Nothing happened.

He yanked it again — and again — and again. The flimsy catch cracked and gave. Jesse pulled open the window.

"We're in!" He grinned. Then, seeing the others stare, "What?"

"Where did you learn to do that?" asked Alice.

"I didn't! I mean, it was obvious. Wasn't it? Oh God, I'm a housebreaker!"

Fergus said, "You are officially no longer Captain Fussypants," and vomited into a flower bed.

One by one, they climbed through the window into a large room with stone floors and thick curtains and sofas arranged before a stove and bookshelves lining the walls. It was, if anything, colder than outside, with the damp and musty smell of a house that has been closed for too long. Fergus sneezed again. A sour, fetid smell reached their nostrils.

"I'm sorry," he croaked. "I couldn't hold it in. The oyster's coming out the other end now."

The living room opened onto a stone passageway, with a door into an old-fashioned farmhouse kitchen, at the end of which they found a utility room with a shower, a washing machine, a tumble dryer, and — thankfully — another door to a toilet. Jesse shoved Fergus inside.

"Do your worst," he said. "I'll get the shower working."

It is surprising how quickly you can adapt to a life of crime when you are desperate. At first, Alice and Jesse tiptoed around the house, hardly daring to touch anything. Little by little, as Calva revealed its marvels, they grew bolder. Jesse found a hot-water switch. He and Alice washed away the worst of the mud and sand and poop and vomit with cold water. Then, once it had heated up, they all showered again for ages. They put their dirty clothes in the washing machine and the clean ones in the tumble dryer with their sleeping bags, and they found bathrobes in the rooms upstairs to wear in the meantime. They had no idea how to make the radiators work, but there were piles of logs by the stove. Shameless now, Jesse built up a fire, and he and Alice made a bed for Fergus in front of it on one of the sofas, with duvets taken from the bedrooms and hot-water bottles found in another bathroom upstairs, and stole tea from the kitchen, brewed it, and made him drink it, spoonful by spoonful, until his teeth stopped chattering. When Fergus had warmed up, Jesse heated a tin of beans and sausages for himself and Alice, with a tin of peaches and one of custard for dessert, all also stolen, while Fergus drank yet more tea and observed that he would probably never eat again.

"But I don't mind," he said. "I used to think that food was an essential source of happiness, but right now I find that not being rained on while trees crash down around you and your body empties itself from every orifice is enough."

Jesse snorted and said they were all relieved about that, and that tomorrow they would try to find a doctor if he was still ill.

"I tried to call, but the telephone line isn't working. Nor is the radio. But they'll probably be all right again tomorrow. If they're not, I'll go into the village."

"And tell them we broke into a house?"

"They'll understand." Jesse sounded uncertain. "We should probably call school too."

The others stared at him, appalled.

"But we're going to the island tomorrow!" cried Alice.

"Alice, Fergus is green!"

"I'm not as green as I was," Fergus argued. There was absolutely no way he was going to let the plan fail because of his parents' habit of eating raw wild shellfish. "I'm getting less green by the minute. Jesse! We've survived a giant storm and a poisonous oyster and that long, long walk. What else could go wrong? This is super-fun, isn't it? I think it's super-fun, and I've just been leaking from my bum and my mouth at the same time."

Alice's gaze turned from horrified to pleading.

"It is fun," Jesse admitted.

"Super-fun," Fergus corrected.

"Mega-super-fun." Jesse smiled.

"So we're all agreed?" Fergus insisted. "We're not going to the doctor, or calling school, or doing anything stupid like that? We're carrying on with the plan?"

Alice nodded vigorously.

"As long as Fergus is better," Jesse warned.

"Oh, I will be better, my friend. I will be one hundred percent absolutely better."

It felt like a step too far to use the bedrooms, so they all lay in their sleeping bags in front of the fire, feeling drowsy but still too full of the day to sleep.

"Do you remember the first time we met?" Fergus yawned. "You would never have thought, would you, that it would all lead to this?"

"I'm not that surprised," Alice said. "You're always getting into trouble, and Jesse—"

"Jesse never gets into trouble—until today, that is, when he's gotten into more trouble than in his entire life. You could never have guessed Jesse would do this."

"Thanks for making me sound so interesting," said Jesse.

"What I was going to say, before you interrupted me, is that Jesse is always looking after people." Alice turned to smile at him. "Remember when you shared your picnic with me on the train?"

Jesse smiled back. Of course he remembered! Euston, his brothers, the first time they'd met—it felt like a lifetime ago. He saw himself again, bowing to the door in his berth, plucking up the courage to explain to her the truth about his peeing habits. "I can't believe I was so embarrassed," he said without thinking, then cursed himself when Fergus asked, "What were you embarrassed about?"

"It doesn't matter. It was silly."

"What was it?"

"I said, it doesn't matter."

"It really doesn't, Fergus," murmured Alice.

"But I want to know! We're a team! We don't have secrets!"

"ONCE WHEN I WAS FIVE MY BROTHERS TICKLED ME AND I PEED IN MY PANTS!" A shocked silence greeted his words. "Sorry," Jesse mumbled. "It's just that sometimes Fergus is so annoying." They laughed so hard they nearly wept, even Jesse. To be honest, they laughed so hard, they all nearly peed. In fact Fergus did pee, just a little bit, though he wouldn't admit it. He'd released enough embarrassing fluids for one day.

It felt good, the laughter, after the day they'd had.

THIRTY-TWO

Issue a Full Description

N0 ONE COULD remember a storm like it at Stormy Loch. Wind howled through the pass and tore a trail of destruction through the woods. Tiles flew off the roof of the boathouse.

The loch growled darkly.

Inside the school, Matron threw economy to the wind and made emergency hot chocolate. And high in his tower, the major spoke on the telephone to Madoc at the youth hostel at Grigaich.

"I've collected almost all the groups," Madoc said. "There's room for all of them to squeeze in here."

"When you say 'almost' . . ."

Madoc winced. "I'm afraid the final group never arrived at their site. They were actually meant to be camping a few miles from here tonight, and should have come through the village, but I've asked everywhere and no one has seen them. Dr. Csintalan and Professor Lawrence have traced their route as far as they can, but there's no sign of them. I've had to call the police."

"Which group is it?"

"Fergus Mackenzie, Alice Mistlethwaite, and Jesse Okuyo."

Well, well, thought the major. Jesse, Fergus, and Alice. Why was he not surprised? He had wondered about the wisdom of putting those three together—two trouble-prone children and one badly in need of breaking a few rules. But he had thought they might help one another. Of course, there was nothing to say they weren't doing so, he reflected as thunder rattled his window and the terrified kittens shot under the sofa. It was only a bit of weather . . . Not exactly a war zone. Another crash of thunder rolled in, and he was reminded that weather can be as dangerous as any enemy. More dangerous sometimes, he thought, remembering a flood in Southeast Asia, an Australian desert fire . . .

"The only potential sighting we have is from a ferryman who took three children to Lumm," said Madoc. "But he thought they were French."

"French!"

"Yes, sir. Two boys and a girl, in orange waterproofs."

"What the blazes are they doing on Lumm? Oh, never mind that! Can you get over there?"

"Not tonight, sir. I've asked. No boats going out in this weather."

The major glanced out the window. "And I doubt I'll get very far either, even in the Land Rover. All right, Madoc. I'll call their families, and then I'll get to you as soon as I can. Meanwhile, I want the police and the coast guard informed and briefed. Issue a full description. Someone must have seen them."

The rain lashed and the wind swept. All over western Scotland, families locked doors and bolted windows and gathered to tell stories. Livestock huddled under trees, birds clung to their nests. From a crowded youth hostel in a small village, Madoc made his calls, and on a windswept coast, Barney Mistlethwaite listened to the sea roar. At an old-fashioned country hotel on Lumm, a small woman dressed in black paced about her room.

In a garden, in a stolen house, three exhausted runaways slept.

What else could go wrong? Fergus had asked.

Quite a lot, my friend. Quite a lot indeed.

THIRTY-THREE

It's That Global Warming

ALICE WOKE WITH a start, certain that she was being watched, and looked fearfully toward the windows, pale in the light of dawn. No one was there. Still she could not shake the feeling. Her nightmare of the empty hallway had returned in the night and left her anxious. When she remembered that today was the day she was to meet Barney, her heart raced even faster.

She checked the time. It was half past five. The boat for Nish left in two hours. Jesse had set an alarm for six. There was no way she could sleep again, or even lie still. Careful not to wake the others, she slid out of her sleeping bag and, taking it with her, went into the utility room to use the bathroom and gather her dry clothes into her rucksack.

And there, at the bottom of her pack, nestling among her socks, was Barney's parcel.

This is not, I'm afraid, the moment when you find out what's inside. Be patient—I promise you'll find out soon. For now, though, Alice just felt the parcel, as she had in her room at school, and tried once again to guess its contents. She did not allow herself to ask why she wasn't allowed to open a parcel addressed to her, or to wonder why Barney, who never wrote so much as a letter, had gone to the trouble of sending it by mail. She knew only that her tummy was so full of butterflies, she felt almost sick.

It was nearly six o'clock. She went back into the living room. The boys were both still deeply asleep. Jesse was on his front, snoring, but Fergus lay on his back. She tiptoed over to look at him. Even in the semi-darkness, she could see that he was still very pale, with bruised smudges under his eyes.

What if he wasn't well enough to travel? Jesse had said they wouldn't go. Alice didn't think she could bear that.

Suddenly, without thinking or weighing up the consequences or all the other things you are supposed to do before making a momentous decision, she made up her mind.

Very carefully, she retrieved Jesse's phone and turned off his alarm, then went back to the utility room, where she dressed as quickly and quietly as she could. She picked up her rucksack. There was a key hanging by the back door. She let herself out, closed the door quietly behind her, and slipped, quite alone, into the garden.

The wind had calmed but the rain had not, and she was glad

for her school waterproofs. The air smelled of earth and damp, and the road and surrounding fields were slick with water. She came to the fallen tree and skirted it, watching every step, keeping her hand on the trunk for safety in case the ground turned into a bog and she sank. She tried not to think of Jesse and Fergus, and their reaction when they woke to find her gone. Already, guilt was sitting heavy alongside the butterflies in her stomach.

She arrived at the quay with half an hour to spare and stood by the water's edge to wait, watching the rise and fall of the waves. These clouds, the low mist, the dark and stormy sea . . . It occurred to her that she still had no idea in which direction Nish lay. Jesse would know, of course, but she didn't want to think about him. She turned her mind instead to Barney, wondering if he was already on Nish, or on his way, or even — the thought struck her like a thunderbolt — about to get on the same boat as her?

She heard footsteps — someone was coming, and now her heart was in her mouth as she imagined . . .

"All right, lass?" It was not Barney, but an old bearded man in heavy oilskins. Alice tried to steady her breathing.

"I'm waiting for the boat to Nish," she told him.

"Waiting for a boat?" The old man shook and his chest wheezed. He seemed to think she was hilarious. "There's no boat to Nish today, lass, nor to anywhere, not even a ferry to the mainland, not with the sea the way she is out there. Did you not hear the storm in the night?"

"N-no boat at all?" stammered Alice.

"It's that global warming, they say," the old man rambled. "Weather getting worse and worse, and oceans rising, and—"

"Until when?" Alice demanded. "Until when are there no boats?"

The old man sniffed at the interruption. "Maybe tomorrow?"

"But I have to go today!"

"Well, you can't." The old man narrowed his eyes. "Shouldn't you be at school?"

Suddenly she realized how suspicious she must look—a girl out alone on a school day, in the driving rain.

"I'm doing a project," she garbled. "For geography. We're . . . we're counting birds!"

And then she turned and fled.

The disappointment was crushing. Alice didn't think she could bear it. She had been so close! She had thought she would see Barney today—had even imagined his footsteps! And where was he now? she wondered miserably. Was he somewhere on Lumm, looking for a boat? Or was he already on the island?

Would he wait for her?

That was the thing with Barney. You just never knew.

Alice started crying as she came out of the village, and could not stop. She cried all the way down the road toward the beach, and she cried as she walked through Calva's tangled garden to the back door, and she cried as she went into the house, and when Fergus and Jesse, barely awake, staggered out of the living room with loud exclamations at the sight of her dripping onto the linoleum floor.

They took off her waterproofs and boots, led her upstairs, ran a bath into which they squeezed gallons of someone else's bubble bath, and boiled water for more hot-water bottles and tea, and put the clothes she handed through the bathroom door back into the tumble dryer. And when she came downstairs, they told her what they had heard, and what they had decided.

THIRTY-FOUR

It Sure Is Different from Oklahoma

SCHOOL KNOWS WE'RE MISSING!" Fergus announced. Alice couldn't believe what she was hearing. "It was on the radio! They described us and everything."

"The police are looking for us," Jesse added. "They know we're here, I mean on Lumm. They're asking for witnesses."

"They called me a white redhead with braces!"

"To be fair . . ." Jesse trailed off, quelled by Fergus's indignant glare. "The point is, we're already in trouble."

"So"—Fergus beat a drumroll on the kitchen table—"we think, when the boats are working again, we might as well go on!"

"What?" Alice, dazed, stared from Fergus to Jesse and then back to Fergus. "But . . ."

"We'll need disguises," Jesse said seriously. "And we'll need to think what to say to school, you know, when we get back. I don't think they'd believe us if we just said we'd got lost, but we could maybe say we really wanted to see puffins."

"From now on," said Fergus, gazing fondly at Jesse, "I'm going to call you Rebel."

"But Dad . . . It was meant to be today . . . I don't know where . . . What if tomorrow's too late?"

"If he's already on Nish, he won't be able to leave," said Jesse. "And if he isn't, the chances are he'll guess you couldn't go today, and he'll go tomorrow too. Probably. I mean, we can't know for sure —"

"But it's worth a try!" cried Fergus.

Alice's mind was racing. School . . . Already in trouble . . . Barney, and the weather . . . It all made sense.

Sort of. It made sense to her, anyway. Except for one thing . . .

"But why?" she asked. "I left you. I turned off Jesse's alarm!"

"That was bad," Fergus admitted. "To be honest, we were furious. Especially Jesse. 'I didn't give up the flipping Orienteering Challenge for Alice to flipping leave us.' That's what you said, isn't it, Jesse?"

Jesse, wishing Fergus weren't quite so free with information, muttered something about the heat of the moment but conceded that yes, he had been kind of cross.

"Furious," Fergus corrected him. "But never mind about that, because that's all over, and we love you. Don't we, Jesse?"

Jesse, blushing, mumbled that they did.

"And so it's decided!" Fergus beamed. "We're going to find your dad, and the castle, and the puffins!"

"Like a quest," said Jesse shyly.

Alice didn't know what to say. She rubbed her eyes and sniffed and stared at the floor to stop herself from crying again, then burst into tears anyway and wailed, "I can't believe you're doing this for me!"

Fergus laughed and squeezed her affectionately. Jesse, over-whelmed by so much emotion, fled to the kitchen to make more tea.

Again, I'm not saying you would do the same thing. You, who I'm sure are a sensible person, would probably say, *Let's not waste the police's time on pursuing this adventure, especially when the outcome is so uncertain,* and also, *Let's be nice and put our school, our parents, our brothers, our aunt, and everyone who cares about us out of their misery, worrying where we are, lost on a camping trip during one of the worst storms in living memory.*

But this is not your story, and Alice, Fergus, and Jesse had much more interesting things to think about. There was a father to find! A plan to mastermind! A whole new island to explore!

"So, the disguises!" Fergus said. "Should I shave my head? Can we take off my braces?"

"You can wear a hat, Fergus." Alice, no longer crying, was riffling through a box of outdoor clothes in the utility room. "Look, here's a beanie—we should all wear hats! And here are ponchos and jackets to wear instead of our orange school things. You'll just have to keep your mouth shut to hide your braces." She grinned. "That might be the hardest thing."

"Rude," said Fergus.

"How did they describe Jesse?"

"Tall and mixed race," said Fergus. "So good luck with that. Perhaps he could pretend to be American. That would confuse people. Jesse, say something American."

"I am not going to do that."

"Jesse!" begged Alice.

"No!"

"He's not made for deceit and subterfuge after all," Fergus whispered. "Probably doesn't even know what the words mean."

"I can hear you, Fergus," Jesse growled. "And I do know what *deceit* and *subterfuge* mean. They mean lying."

"Rules are rules." Fergus sighed. "You're a useless criminal. Probably not even a very good explorer."

Jesse glared at him. "HOWDY!" he thundered. "HOW Y'ALL DOIN' TODAY? IT SURE IS DIFFERENT HERE FROM OKLAHOMA!"

"Oklahoma?" said Alice.

Fergus grinned. "Do you think real Americans would actually say that?"

"I SWEAR ONE DAY I'M GOING TO KILL YOU!"

"No you won't." Fergus jammed a pink fleecy hat on his head. "You love me. You love both of us. That's why you're doing this. That, and the exploring practice."

We are nearly at the moment now when everything comes together — the runaways on their quest, the people chasing them, Barney, the police, the major. That troublesome parcel in Alice's rucksack . . . You can see just by looking at your book that we are nearly there — wherever there may be.

But that's all for tomorrow.

Today, Alice and Fergus and Jesse are going to raid Calva for more food. They are going to take books to read from its well-stocked shelves and find a pack of playing cards, and Jesse is going to teach the others games he learned from his brothers. Later, when the rain stops, they are going to go to the beach and race along the surf and chase each other with strands of seaweed washed up by the storm.

This evening, Fergus will perfect their disguises, and Jesse will write a conscientious list for the owners of Calva detailing everything they have taken, promising to reimburse food, pay for electricity, and return clothes. Alice will curl up on the sofa and try to write an adventure about pirates and islands and maybe magical seals, but she will realize for the first time in her life that right now she is not much interested in making up a story.

Instead, she will sit happily by the fire, watching the flames dance and listening to the boys' good-natured squabble, and she will think how strange it is that this stolen house, to which she came only yesterday and which she will leave again tomorrow, should feel like home.

THIRTY-FIVE

Rome

THE BOAT FOR Nish was small, with a sheltered cabin and four wooden benches at the fore, and an open deck with additional seating at the aft. The three had agreed to split up, to reduce suspicion. Alice and Fergus boarded first and made for seats right at the back, where she pretended to read a book and he hid his face behind a discarded newspaper he had retrieved out of a trash can in the terminal as a useful prop. Jesse strolled on with half a dozen brightly dressed Spanish students, behind an Indian family and before an elderly Australian man with a big camera.

"Do you think he looks American?" Fergus whispered. "Because he's not actually saying anything."

"Stop staring at him!" Alice hissed. "Look at the water, or the sky, or, I don't know—a fish! Just don't talk, or someone will see your braces."

Fergus sighed and went back to his newspaper.

Please don't recognize us, Alice prayed, holding her breath. *Please please please . . .*

There were no more passengers left to board. The captain tooted the horn twice, the Spanish students cheered—a spotty youth in oilskin overalls was casting off, a woman and a little girl on the quayside were waving . . . They were off!

Alice breathed again.

She did not see the woman dressed in black, watching through binoculars from the hill behind the quay.

Please let Dad be there, Alice prayed now. *Please please please . . .*

Beside her, Fergus yelped, "Alice!"

"Shhh!"

Lips clamped, still holding the paper high to hide his face, Fergus pointed to a headline with his chin.

LEOPARD SPOTTED ON BRITISH SOIL!

"Since when are you interested in wildlife?" murmured Alice. Fergus's chin swung left to point at a picture. It was not a good shot. It was grainy and patchy, and the newspaper's previous owner had spilled a drink on it before putting it in the trash, but even so, two things were obvious.

It was not a picture of a leopard, but of a woman. And it was a picture of the woman in black. Alice's heart thudded as she leaned in to read the article.

Notorious cat burglar Giovanna Lambetti, commonly known as Il Leopardo (the Leopard), has been sighted on the Inner Hebridean island of Lumm. Lambetti was until recently the lead suspect in the case of the sensational theft of an invaluable Chinese artifact, stolen from a sealed room at the home of billionaire art collector Sergio Grimaldi. She has also been questioned in connection with an attack on Signor Grimaldi's son, Nero, but released without charge due to lack of evidence.

What brings the Leopard to our northern shores? Is it just tourism? Or is she on the hunt? If so, beware—we hear she's been known to eat her victims! One thing's for sure—she's not here for the weather!

It was a silly, sensational article in a rag of a paper, but it sent shivers down Alice's spine. It reminded her of something, but she couldn't think what.

"It's the woman who missed the ferry," Fergus whispered.

"I know."

"A notorious cat burglar!" Fergus scanned the article again. "And she was almost on our boat! This is thrilling. Alice! Why don't you look thrilled?"

"I'm trying to remember something." Thoughts jumbled through Alice's mind, random memories trying to force themselves into a pattern, but still so disconnected, something to do with Tatiana driving, and Jesse's brothers on Visitors' Day, and Jesse scowling, and Tatiana all smiles . . . *I am definitely taking them out in my Maserati when I win that million* . . .

That was it—a reward! The radio, on her first day at Stormy Loch, driving from Castlehaig to school—a million-euro reward for a small jade figurine, stolen from a private home in Rome!

It was all coming back to her—and with it a mounting sense of dread.

Rome . . . and an Italian thief, staring at her on a Scottish quay . . .

Rome . . . where Barney had sent his letter from . . .

Italy . . . where the parcel had come from . . .

So here we are. On a boat, on the Scottish seas, surrounded by Spanish and Indian and Australian tourists, about to discover what an Englishman sent from Italy to his half-Polish daughter . . .

Alice's fingers shook as she fumbled with the clips and drawstring of her rucksack, as she pushed aside socks and fleeces and underwear until she found the small yellow padded mailer tightly bound with brown tape. Still shaking, she unzipped the rucksack's hood, flicked open her small penknife. The tape did not give easily but clung to the blade as she sawed. She kept her hands buried in the rucksack as she worked, aware that no one must see what she was doing. Inside the bag was a layer of bubble wrap, and inside the bubble wrap, a small box, and inside the box, buried in straw . . .

"Fergus," she whispered. "Is there a picture of the thing that was stolen?"

He nodded, and held out the paper.

Alice's world turned upside down.

"Alice, what's wrong?"

Eyes wide, she nodded at him to look inside her rucksack.

"It's too dark," he said. "I can't see."

She raised her hand closer to the light, still shielding it from view.

Nestling in Alice's palm lay a small jade carving of a boy astride a dragon, no bigger than a plum.

The figurine was beautiful, intricately wrought, pale green and almost luminous and surprisingly warm. The boy, riding with his head thrown back, made you want to dance for joy and ride a dragon of your own.

The dragon, despite being tiny, rippled with power and danger and strength. It had been carved, the newspaper informed a stunned Fergus and Alice, in the middle of the nineteenth century, a present to the current owner's grandfather during a visit to China. The sculptor's identity was unknown. There was no piece like it anywhere in the world. There was, as we know, a million-euro reward. No questions would be asked of the person who returned the carving.

Most important of all, as far as our story is concerned, it was in Alice's rucksack.

On they sailed under the pale blue sky, sunlight glinting off the waves. It was impossible to believe there had ever been a storm. They passed an island of black cliff faces wreathed in gulls and guillemots, and another the size of the sports field at school. The Australian took photographs, the Indian family ate their picnic, the Spanish students listened to music on one another's headphones. Jesse, sitting alone at the fore, studied a map. Alice and Fergus, oblivious to all this, stared at the yellow padded mailer into which Alice had returned the carving and had a low, panicked argument.

"What is it doing here?" hissed Fergus.

"I don't know! Dad sent it! He asked me to bring it."

"Why didn't you tell us there was a parcel?"

"I never even thought about it!"

That was a lie and they both knew it.

"We have to turn it in," insisted Fergus. "We have to go straight back and find the police."

"And say what?"

"I don't know! I'm not exactly an expert in this kind of thing. Anyway, look . . . read! It says 'No questions asked.'"

"There are always questions asked," Alice said. "Especially when you're a kid."

"But the Leopard woman—she must be after it!" Fergus gasped. "Alice, she pointed at you—she must know who you are! We have to go to the police! We'll just tell them we found it on a beach."

"Like they'll believe that!"

Just as he was about to demand, exasperated, whether she had a better idea, she turned to him and said, in quiet desperation, "Oh, Fergus . . . Dad!"

She had risked so much to find Barney because she needed so badly to believe that he wanted her—that this was one of those mad escapades that made them who they were, Barney and Alice, father and daughter. And now—she couldn't believe he had just been using her to bring him a stolen statue. She wouldn't believe he was a thief.

"There has to be some explanation," she said miserably.

Fergus's astonishment, his exasperation, his panic all deserted him and another emotion took their place. It took him a while to identify it, and when he did, he was surprised at how strong it was.

Clenched teeth. Short breath. Every muscle in his body tense. He was furious.

Alice's father was using her, and she didn't deserve this.

Fergus was upset with Alice for not telling him about the parcel. But he was furious with Barney Mistlethwaite.

Two hours and thirty-five minutes after leaving Lumm, they docked at a floating jetty off a small sandy beach on Nish. Tidal mudflats stretched out behind the beach, patrolled by scurrying gray and white plovers and sedate red-beaked oystercatchers, digging for food before the rising tide reclaimed the land. Beyond, a path led through short grass up a cliff to the rest of the island.

"You have one hour," said the captain as they filed off the boat. "You'll see the island dips in the middle. There's a sign. Don't pass it. If you're on the wrong side of it at high tide, there's no way of getting you back without calling out the coast guard."

Jesse had gone on ahead of them, still maintaining the pretense that they weren't together. He deliberately walked slowly, letting all the other passengers pass, and waited for them at a bend in the path at the foot of the cliff, hidden from view by sharp, jagged rocks.

"So," snarled Fergus to Alice as they approached him. "How are you going to tell him?"

But Jesse had news of his own, and he gave it before Alice could speak.

"I looked and looked on the map," he said. "But I couldn't find it. I even asked the captain. There is no castle on the Isle of Nish."

THIRTY-SIX

There Must Be a Castle

WHAT DO YOU mean, no castle?" Fergus cried. "The castle's the whole point!"

"There is no castle on the Isle of Nish," Jesse repeated. "There never has been. We're in the wrong place."

They both looked, rather accusingly, at Alice.

No castle! Alice's world had flipped again but somehow was still not the right way up. No castle made no sense! Feverishly, she went over all the steps that had led her here—the research in the library, Barney's letter, so cryptic, so short—could she have misunderstood it? But what other island could it be? There had been only one conversation about Scotland, she was sure of it . . . she thought . . .

"Th-there must be a c-castle," she stammered. "Dad said!"

"What?" said Fergus nastily. "The same dad who—"

"Shut up, Fergus!" It came out as a shriek, surprising them all.

"Who what?" asked Jesse, looking slowly from Alice to Fergus. "What's going on?"

"Alice will tell you," snarled Fergus.

At first, Alice thought she couldn't do it. Jesse, whom she had all but tricked into coming—who had, she supposed, trusted her, as she had trusted Barney—how could she tell him that her father was a thief? That the danger they faced was much, much graver than any Consequence the major might issue for what now seemed like a silly schoolish prank?

But fears, as the major would say, must be confronted. And so the three sat on the ground, and Alice produced the little carving from her rucksack and told Jesse everything, and afterwards they carried on sitting, looking down toward the wooden jetty and the boat anchored in the harbor, and nobody knew quite what to say because this was not a situation life really prepares you for.

Once the first shock had passed, Jesse tried to be practical. Like Fergus, his first thought was to go to the police. If this Leopard woman was after them, they were in danger, he said. This was a woman who attacked people—maybe even ate them! And those men on the quay had looked mean. Inwardly, he felt bewildered: A priceless Chinese artifact? An infamous cat burglar? Alice's dad somehow involved?

Jesse, unlike Fergus, had never questioned her claims about

her father. He had believed Alice's dad was an up-and-coming actor. He had even believed that the man was interested in birds. He was disappointed too, as well as shocked, because even though he hadn't asked for it, he was loving their adventure, and for it to end like this was . . . sad. Knights and heroes, he suspected, would not go running to the police, or surrender priceless treasures so easily. But those were knights, with swords and armor and horses, whereas he and Alice and Fergus were kids. He gave one regretful look at the unclimbed cliff, the unexplored island, and stood up.

"Come on," he said. "We'll go back to the boat. We'll be safe there."

He held out his hand. Alice stood, meekly, and took it. Sighing, she turned and followed him back down the hill.

Fergus could take it no more. Seeing Alice like this! So dejected, and small—his Alice, whom he had seen stand on rooftops with her arms outstretched to the sky! Who had rowed out into the middle of lochs and let off fireworks, who could make Fergus's blood freeze with the telling of a simple story she made up in her head! Barney Mistlethwaite was a crook, he thought furiously. He didn't deserve a daughter like her, and he, Fergus Mackenzie, wanted to look him in the eye and tell him so.

"Stop!" he shouted. "We're going on!"

The others turned and stared uncomprehendingly.

"But there isn't even a castle!" Alice said.

"There's always a castle. You just have to look for it."

"And what about the Leopard?" Jesse cried.

Fergus spun round, arms wide, palms toward the sky. "Look around you, my friend—there are no leopards in Scotland!"

"But it's dangerous!"

"Do you want an adventure or not?" Fergus shouted. "Come on, Jesse! Call yourself an explorer? This is for Alice! It's important!"

As he turned to face the cliff, he told himself that this was possibly the stupidest thing he had ever done.

Were they brave, or just reckless? Alice wasn't sure. She only knew as she trudged up the path after Fergus to the top of the cliff that she was afraid. What if the Leopard woman found them? What if Barney wasn't here? What if—this was confusing —he *was* here? What would she say to him? Climbing behind her, Jesse tried to focus only on logistics—the boat that left in an hour, the rising tide and the line they must not cross, the castle that did not exist.

Fergus thought nothing, but marched to the rhythm of his rage.

As the dirt path turned to stone, and the stone path turned to steps carved out of rock, and the world was reduced to black walls and the bright blue sky above, Jesse's heart began to beat a little faster with almost unbearable curiosity. Fergus's rage settled into something more like determination.

Alice's fear remained.

They emerged from their climb onto a kind of plateau, with sheer drops on either side. To the right, a short distance away, the rest of the boat party sat strung along the cliff, looking out to sea, like sentinels of nowhere.

"What are they doing?" asked Jesse.

"Watching for birds, I guess," said Fergus. "That is the main point of this trip, for most people."

"But why are they all exactly here?"

The Australian raised his camera, and they heard a whirr of clicks. Curious, they approached the edge of the cliff.

Puffins! Puffins everywhere! Puffins waddling like little fat men going to weddings in black and white suits, puffins watching with their heads cocked to the side, puffins performing a sort of aerial ballet, rising and falling over the edge of the cliffs on the thermals. The runaways stood on the grass at the end of the line of watchers, and Fergus yelped as a bird shot out of the ground between his legs and soared over the edge of the cliff before diving at breakneck speed straight into the waves below.

Even Alice laughed.

"What's it doing underground?" cried Fergus.

"It's where they nest." The Australian had wandered over to

them with his camera. "They spend most of their lives at sea, but come to land to lay their eggs in underground burrows."

"That is so cool." Fergus knelt on the grass to peer down the burrow. An angry striped beak poked out and squawked at him. "So cool."

It was . . . joyous. As joyous as the carved Chinese boy, riding his jade dragon. But there was nothing here—not a wall or stone—that once could have been a castle, and the boat left in less than an hour.

"Come on," said Fergus.

They pressed on.

The Australian with the camera watched them disappear beyond a headland on the end of the plateau. He had a niggling sense that he was missing something. There had been something on the radio this morning, at his hotel. He hadn't paid attention, but he was almost certain it had something to do with three missing children . . .

THIRTY-SEVEN

Knights and Dragons
and Witches

THE GROUND SLOPED away at the end of the headland, and they saw that Nish was like a figure eight, two fat circles that met in the middle where the land narrowed to a few meters across. The lowest point was barely above sea level, and already damp with the rising tide.

"There's the Keep Out sign," said Jesse. "This must be where the captain meant when he said don't go any farther."

"That's it, then." Alice felt a rush of relief, followed by a sting of disappointment. It was obvious they could not continue. There was nothing for it but to go back to the boat, and safety, and school—but she could not help thinking that this was somehow running away and hiding.

Which, of course, is sometimes the wisest thing to do.

Sometimes. Depending on whether you're being reckless or brave.

"Oh for God's sake!" Jesse cried. "FERGUS, COME BACK!"

Alice, dragged back from her thoughts, saw that Fergus had already leaped over the divide.

"The castle must be on this side of the island," he shouted. "That's why no one knows about it!"

"ALICE, THERE IS NO CASTLE!" Jesse yelled. "AND WE'RE NOT SUPPOSED TO GO PAST HERE AND THE TIDE IS COMING IN AND WE'LL BE CUT OFF!"

"YOU STAY, THEN! I'M GOING ON!"

They went on.

The going was less steady now, the ground more rugged. They walked around one headland, then another. Jesse glanced nervously at his watch. In another thirty minutes, the boat would leave.

Sooner than that, the tide would cut them off.

They came to a path that hugged the edge of a cliff much higher than on the other side of the island, with a choppier sea below. Alice's vertigo returned. She felt the familiar blurring of her vision, the growing numbness of her limbs. Dumbly, she held out a hand. Wordlessly, Jesse took it.

She must not look down . . . She must not let the vertigo win . . . Round another headland they went, the path began to dip, and suddenly, they were in a different world.

Guillemots and shags, razorbills and gulls — perched, diving, shrieking, soaring. This was a land as far from the human world as it was possible to be—a place of rock and gullies, of swirling water and foaming spray, of wingbeat and feather. Opposite, joined to the mainland by a narrow spit of beach, stood an eroded arch of rock.

It was primitive, and majestic, and epic.

"Beautiful," breathed Alice, forgetting her vertigo.

"Scary," admitted Fergus.

"It reminds me of a book I read," said Jesse. "It was about King Arthur. It had pictures that looked just like this, but with dragons and knights and witches and . . . Alice!"

"What?"

"And a castle—a castle, on a rock, in the sea!"

Alice froze.

"There's a way up from the beach." Jesse was looking through his binoculars. "At the foot of the arch's first pillar. It's steep, and a bit of a climb, but it's definitely a way up. Alice! I think we've found the castle!"

"Well, don't get too excited," said Fergus in a strangled voice. "Because I think the knights and witch have found us."

Alice and Jesse turned to look behind them. Two men in black and a tiny woman with mosquito sunglasses were running toward them across the grass.

One of the men was carrying a gun.

THIRTY-EIGHT

The Tide Will Go Out

ALICE, FERGUS, AND JESSE ran the only way possible—straight along the path winding tightly down the cliff to a scrap of pebbly beach, already almost submerged by the incoming waves. Jesse, running ahead, glanced over his shoulder and saw that their pursuers were gaining on them, the tiny Leopard running as easily as her henchmen. He stumbled, and pain shot through his ankle. Heedless, he ran on toward the beach, where the tide was rushing in faster than he had ever seen.

Once upon a time, Jesse would have cursed Fergus for his stubbornness, or Alice for being so trusting of her father, and fate for being so unfair to him, but he was discovering a new talent on this trip: the ability to act fast under pressure. Faced with real danger, he thought only of how to get them out of it. He reached the beach and ran straight into the water, gasping as the current threatened to knock him over. Wedging his boots under a boulder, he held out his arms, grabbed Alice as she ran in after him, and swung her toward the fast-disappearing beach at the foot of the arch.

"Find the way up!" he shouted, before turning back for Fergus. "Round the other side—you'll see a fall of rocks, and then some grass."

Unlike Jesse, Fergus was panicking, his anger toward Barney now turned on himself for insisting they carry on. He stifled a sob as he splashed into the water, lost his footing, and fell. The current picked him up. A rock slammed into his way. On the beach, a man in black raised his gun . . .

The shot's echo bounced from cliff to cliff.

Alice screamed. Fergus slumped, blood pouring from his face. Jesse, now in water up to his waist, waded toward him and staggered under his weight, his ankle almost giving way beneath him.

Three more steps . . . two . . . one . . . The boys collapsed onto dry land.

"They're coming over!" Alice was running to them, and they all looked toward the main island to see the gunman wading toward them. "We have to run!"

"Where to?" Fergus shouted. "Where can we possibly run to?"

There was no answer to this. They were stranded on a rock with nowhere to hide and a man coming after them with a gun.

Suddenly, Alice saw what she must do. She struggled out of her rucksack and began to undo the straps.

"What are you doing?" cried Fergus.

"I'm going to give them the carving," she said.

She wondered if this was what the major had meant about becoming fearless through facing fears. She was astonished at how calm she felt.

She opened the top of the rucksack, found Barney's mailer, and pulled out the box containing the carving of the boy and the dragon.

"You go on," she said. "Just in case, you know, they shoot again."

This was absolutely the right thing to do, she told herself. This whole situation was her fault. Barney was her father. She was the one who had got the boys into this mess.

"Don't be stupid!" It was Jesse's turn now to be furious, as Alice apparently failed to understand the danger they were in. "No one's leaving you here with them! What do you think will happen, you'll just hand over the carving and they'll be all, 'Oh, thank you so much, Alice, sorry for all the trouble'? THEY SHOT FERGUS!"

"Guys, calm down." Fergus pointed to the water. "It's too late. They're not going to make it."

The gunman had fallen, was clinging to the same rock that

moments ago had saved Fergus, but the body of sea between him and the children was too great now, and there was no hope of a crossing. The other man in black was inching toward him along the foot of the cliff, holding his hand out to drag him to safety. The gunman seized it, fell again, grasped a rock, and hauled himself onto it and from there to what was left of the beach, where he lay on the pebbles, his gun ripped from his hand by the sea.

Alice put the little box in her pocket.

Away from the shore, they sat Fergus against some boulders, gave him water to drink and soggy chocolate to eat, and carefully cleaned his face.

"Where did he hit you?" Alice asked. "Fergus, answer me!"

"I don't think he did," said Fergus. "I don't know, because I've never been shot before, but I think it would probably hurt much more."

"But the blood . . ."

"I hit my head." Chocolate and water were helping Fergus remember. "It's possible I'm suffering from concussion, and it really stings, but I don't think I'm going to die. Not murdered, anyway. Alice! It's nice to be hugged, but you're hurting me. Guys, I'm sorry—this is all my fault."

"Your fault!" cried Alice. "It's *my*—"

"There's no time for this." Jesse was already thinking about the next step. He hoisted his pack onto his back and began to lead the way round the pillar to the path.

"You're limping!" cried Alice.

"I twisted my ankle looking back at the Leopard," he said shortly. "It's nothing."

"Can't we rest?" Now that the immediate panic was past, Fergus felt utterly exhausted. "The tide's in. They can't touch us."

In the past, Jesse might have rolled his eyes. Now, very calmly, he said, "The tide will go out again."

The others gulped.

"So . . . we have to try and find Alice's father," said Fergus. "And hope that he can help us. And if we don't find him, or he can't . . ."

"I guess then we negotiate with the Leopard."

None of this was reassuring.

It would have been a challenging climb under any circumstances. In wet clothes, carrying heavy packs, with a twisted ankle and a cut forehead and mounting vertigo, they thought it might kill them. The route Jesse had identified was not a path— just grassy ground, winding round the pillar like a steep staircase, sometimes open to the sky, sometimes sheltered by slabs of stone —always with the thrashing sea below. But none of them complained, just as they had not complained what felt like a lifetime ago, on the long walk through the fern forest along the edge of the deer field.

They had come a long way since that first orienteering exercise at Stormy Loch.

THIRTY-NINE

On the Bright White Sand

T HE PATH, SUCH as it was, ended abruptly at a vertical rock face, the height of a two-story house, covered in yellow lichen and white stuff Jesse said was probably centuries of bird droppings.

There was an opening in the rock just wide enough to squeeze through. They shuffled forward. The ground sloped downward, the sky grew smaller, the air was cold.

"We are going into the bowels of the earth," observed Fergus, to defuse the tension.

"Shut up, Fergus," said Jesse.

Another twist, and the sky widened, and now the tunnel was a cave, and the cave was flooded with light. Alice tumbled out first and—just for a moment—felt her heart soar.

Pow! Zap! Take that!

Here was Barney's castle.

A sunken area of grass, like the courtyard of a ruined medieval keep, with four tall rocks marking corners like watchtowers, joined by battlements of stone. Along the wall facing the open sea, a higher embankment of grass just beneath the battlements, like a promenade reached by a staircase of fallen boulders.

The boys emerged from the tunnel.

"We've found it!" Alice said.

They shrugged off their packs. Fergus began to climb the battlement. Jesse, grimacing, sat on the grass and removed his boots.

"I don't see it," he said. "And my ankle's turning black."

"It is a castle." Alice ran to the middle of the courtyard. She could see it so clearly! Barney, running along the embankment, a stick for a sword, defending his island kingdom. The image morphed with a memory: she and Barney as medieval knights, chasing each other through the garden at Cherry Grange, and a hundred other games of make-believe — playing at pirates on the beach, jumping out of hiding as highwaymen on country walks . . .

She smiled. "It's so obvious."

"Then, where's your dad?" Jesse, still barefoot, was limping around the edges of the courtyard, peering into the fissures and hollows of the stone battlements, as if at any moment they might reveal a father.

They had to face the evidence. Barney was not here, and they were too late. They had no hope of getting out before the Leopard caught up with them.

"I'll go back down," said Alice dully. "I mean it, Jesse. I'll go and I'll wait for the Leopard, and I'll give her the carving, and then we'll go back to the boat and—"

"The boat won't be there," Jesse said. "It had to leave before the tide. And I don't know if I can even walk anymore. Alice—I don't think I can do it."

He closed his eyes, feeling utterly defeated, and Alice could have wept for having done this to her friend.

"We'll be fine," she whispered. "You'll think of something. We'll manage, together! Jesse, you're a great explorer!"

"I'm not," he whispered back. "I think maybe I'm just a kid."

There's no such thing as just a kid, she wanted to say, and *You can be a kid and an explorer at the same time,* and also just *Thank you.* But as she struggled to find the words, a great cry went up from the castle's battlements.

"Alice! Alice, up here!"

She looked up, and felt a lurch of vertigo at the sight of Fergus waving from the embankment, silhouetted against the sky.

"Alice, you idiot, come and see!"

Breath by breath, she climbed the battlement. Crawling, she

approached the edge of the embankment. With a whimper, she dragged herself up to kneeling, to peer over the edge . . .

Fergus jumped.

Alice screamed, then laughed.

There was land on the other side. Flat land, flowers, a wide grassy path sloping gently, manageably, toward a low cliff, and clear, dark blue water beyond.

"Jump!" shouted Fergus.

She jumped and followed him carefully to the edge of the cliff. A cove began to appear, and . . .

"A boat?"

"Not only a boat—look! You have to look straight down!"

She held tightly to his hand. Driven into the top of the cliff was a spike, and tied to the spike was a rope, and at the bottom of the rope, on the bright white sand . . .

"Dad's arrived!" Alice yelled. "Dad! DAD!"

The wind danced away her voice.

"MR. MISTLETHWAITE!"

Barney jumped as a stone, thrown by Fergus, landed with a splash beside him.

He looked up. Alice waved, clinging to Fergus.

"Dad! Dad, we're here too! We all made it!"

Barney whooped and waved back, then ran to the rope and began to climb.

FORTY

The Actor

ALICE FLEW INTO her father's arms. For a while, there was nothing else in the world. No unanswered emails or canceled visits, no Leopard woman or Chinese figurine—no questions. Only Barney, and his arms holding her tight, and the wonderful, familiar smell of lemon and leather, and a warm glow as he said, "You found it! You clever girl, you found it!"

But they were in danger, and the moment was short-lived. As Fergus glared from a short distance away and Jesse dragged himself over the battlement to join them, Alice gabbled, "Dad, we have to go!" just as Barney, a little wildly, said, "There are three of you!"

He wasn't pleased. Fergus and Jesse saw it immediately, even if Alice didn't, and exchanged worried glances. Fergus stepped in closer, protectively. Jesse, his ankle throbbing, sat on the ground and contemplated their next move.

"These are my friends!" Alice said breathlessly. "Fergus and Jesse. They're amazing, Dad! They . . ."

Jesse stopped listening. Something wasn't right. It wasn't just Barney's reaction to him and Fergus—that was almost to be expected, given the circumstances of the carving. No, it was more than that . . . He looked down at the beach, Barney's boat, the little cove . . . He frowned.

The entrance to the cove was guarded by stacks similar to the pillars of the arch they had just climbed to get away from the Leopard, which meant . . .

"Can you only sail in and out at high tide?" Jesse asked.

"Excuse me?" Barney sounded impatient, but Jesse persevered.

"This is a secret cove, like in pirate stories," he said. "There's only one way in. But if it's like the other side, that must mean that at low tide there's no way out."

He looked down at Barney's boat. He saw now that there was a rucksack in the boat. Like Alice, he had assumed that Barney had just arrived. But if that were the case, his shoes, or at least the bottom of his trousers, would be wet from pulling the boat ashore—wouldn't they? And then there was this spike driven into the cliff, this rope . . . Had they been here a while, set up by previous visitors to the castle rock? Or had Barney brought them?

Jesse wriggled closer. The rope looked new, the spike shiny and unweathered. Which meant, probably, that Barney had driven it in, which in turn meant that he had not just arrived, which therefore meant . . .

"Were you actually leaving, Mr. Mistlethwaite?"

"I . . ." Barney hesitated. Three pairs of eyes were trained on him—the boys' hostile, Alice's wide and uncomprehending. "I . . . The thing is . . . Alicat, my letter, the date . . . I was expecting you yesterday!"

Watching Barney squirm, Fergus felt his rage return. Was this the man Alice hero-worshipped and protected? "Th-there was a s-storm," she was stammering—as if she needed to make excuses, when the whole world knew there had been a storm.

"Never mind all that." Jesse, once again, took control. "We just have to leave, now. On Barney's boat. We can explain everything later."

"Oh, I'm not going anywhere," said Fergus.

"Fergus, there's no time for this!" cried Jesse. "The tide! The flipping Leopard!"

Barney went pale. "The Leopard?"

"Oh, didn't we say?" snarled Fergus. "She shot us . . ."

". . . and she's trying to get here," finished Jesse. "So, Fergus, SHUT UP and—"

"I am not going anywhere," Fergus repeated, surprised at his own determination. "Not until he tells us about the carving."

And there it was.

Relationships change, all the time. Mostly, you don't see the change until it's happened. But sometimes, if you pay attention, you recognize moments after which nothing is ever the same— an apology unspoken, a handshake ignored, a lie discovered . . .

A trust, broken.

Barney went very still, then turned to Alice.

"You opened it?"

"Yes."

She couldn't tell if he looked sad or guilty or disappointed or angry, or a combination of all four.

Until now, Alice had secretly still been clinging to the hope of a mistake. In a story, an evil villain would have tricked Barney into sending the carving—or this boy and dragon would be a fake—or Barney would have been blackmailed, or working for the secret service, or . . .

This was not a story. And Barney's "You opened it?" con- firmed all that Alice had feared.

She had been standing near her father. Now, almost uncon- sciously, she edged away from him toward Jesse, still watching the sea on the edge of the cliff.

"I think Alice deserves to know why you sent her that thing," said Fergus coldly. "Also, why you made her bring it here. I mean, what sort of person does that? What sort of useless parent . . ."

"All right, all right!" Barney threw up his hands. Fergus

grunted and went to sit beside Alice. Jesse, sighing, felt inside his jacket pocket for a very damp map of the island. Alice, her throat a painful lump, shuffled right up to him as she watched her father.

"There's this guy called Nero," Barney said. "He's Signor Grimaldi's son. I met him years ago when I was touring in Italy."

Fergus, at the mention of theatrical touring, snorted. Alice shushed him anxiously.

"I met him at a card game—a small thing, just Sunday-afternoon café stuff—I don't play big stakes at cards." Barney shot a concerned look at Alice, as if trying to reassure her. Again, Fergus snorted. Barney sighed. "Well, Nero does love gambling. A few weeks ago, he met this Canadian guy who plays for big money. And Nero lost—a lot. And it turns out . . ."

Barney paused. Fergus, despite himself, leaned forward.

"What?"

"It turns out Canadians aren't all as nice as they seem. This one threatened to go to Signor Grimaldi when Nero said he couldn't pay what he owed. And Nero really didn't want that, because the last time his dad paid off his debts, he warned him he wouldn't do it again. So that's why Nero took the carving."

"He stole it from his own father?" Fergus sounded fascinated now rather than cross, and Alice's feelings were all over the place —relief that Barney hadn't actually stolen the boy and dragon, but also an unsettling sense that he was enjoying this far too much—as if, rather than making a confession, he were putting on a show.

"Excuse me," Jesse said. "The tide . . ."

They ignored him.

"It's not really stealing," Barney argued. "More like an advance on Nero's inheritance. And it's not like anyone was actually hurt. So anyway, Nero disabled the CCTV and took the carving, then advised his dad to offer a reward, no questions asked. And that's where I come in—the Englishman unconnected to any of this, who just 'happened' upon the statue, and an actor! It was all going great, until that idiot Nero panicked, said he'd been attacked, and tried to pin the theft on the Leopard. That changed everything. She's been trying to find the carving ever since the police let her go, and when her spies discovered I had it, she came after me. That's why I got the idea of sending it to your school—I figured no one would go looking for it there. I was going to pick it up when I came to visit, but then I heard the Leopard was in the UK, and decided I couldn't risk it."

He turned to Alice. "I wish I could have come to your school, sweetheart. Then all of this could have been avoided."

And, perhaps, that was the biggest betrayal of all.

A painful lump was forming in Alice's throat. All this, she thought—giving him a final chance, tricking school, all this!

Fergus's illness, the storm, his head wound, Jesse's ankle, the Orienteering Challenge—her promise to the major! Wanting to believe he wanted to show her the island! It did not seem to have occurred to Barney how much danger he had put them in.

She looked at him more closely, and something shifted, as if she were seeing a different Barney—almost the same as ever, but unshaven, the smell of lemon overlaid with sweat, dark rings beneath the bright blue eyes . . . He had betrayed her, and all the trust she had ever put in him, because she had been too afraid to look the truth in the face—that Barney could never be trusted and would never be there when she needed him.

"What happened next?" Fergus was still riveted.

"Well, now that Alice has brought the carving—you have got it, Alicat, haven't you?—once everything has calmed down a bit, I'll shimmy on back to Italy, we'll get the money, Nero'll pay his debts, and hey presto! Daddy's rich!" He grinned. "Clever, no?"

"For heaven's sake!" Jesse yelled. "Am I literally the only one here who has been watching the tide?"

"The tide?" Fergus, jolted suddenly from Barney's story back to reality, looked dazed.

"It's going out! And another thing—has it not occurred to anyone else that the Leopard must have a boat?" He laid out his map, ignoring the others' baffled panic. "She might be here"—he pointed—"at the beach where we landed, in which case until the tide goes down enough she's cut off from it. But she could also have landed here"—more pointing—"or even here, on this side of the cutoff, in which case she could already be on her way. So we need to go now."

Alice stared blankly as Jesse started issuing orders. "Mr. Mistlethwaite," he said, "you should go first to show us how it's done. Alice, you'll go next—don't worry, I'll talk you down—then me, so Fergus can help with my ankle. You'll have to lower the packs too. Is that OK? Great. Then let's get our rucksacks from the castle, and LET'S GO!"

Really, thank goodness for Jesse.

Fergus ran for the packs. Barney grabbed the rope and bounced down the cliff.

Alice did not move.

She was thinking of a story.

A story that needed an ending.

FORTY-ONE

And the Sky Exploded

ONCE UPON A TIME, *there was a house in a garden full of cherry trees, and the little girl who lived in that house was the happiest girl in the world. In summer she could pick cherries straight off the tree outside her bedroom window, and one spring night, when the tree was a cloud of pink flowers, she tried to sleep in it because it was just how she imagined a princess's castle . . .*

Jesse and Fergus watched, concerned. "What's she doing?" Jesse asked. "Why is she just sitting there?"

"I think . . ." Fergus narrowed his eyes. Alice sat staring into space, absolutely still except for . . . her left hand, gently twitching. "I think she's writing."

o   o   o

The little girl's mother wouldn't let her sleep in the tree,
and ordered her back inside. But secretly, she hoped her
daughter would always be

Alice stood up, her chin set at its most stubborn angle.

She knew the story's ending.

"Now what?" Jesse whispered.

Fergus shrugged. "I don't know!"

Alice, steely-voiced, said, "Show me how I get down."

"Whatever you do, do not just slide down the rope, or you'll burn your hands." Jesse peppered Alice with instructions as she prepared to go over the top of the cliff. "One hand over the other, and keep your legs braced. It's not too high, so if you fall, you might break a leg, but you're unlikely to die. Oh, and don't look down."

Alice had intended to be fearless. She didn't feel it now. The drop beneath her made her want to howl. Or hide. Or be sick. Or all three together.

And this wasn't even the most frightening thing she had to confront.

"Way to help, Jesse," said Fergus. "She's gone green."

"That's not helping either," Jesse said reprovingly. "Alice, you OK?"

She gripped the rope with both hands and slid over the edge of the cliff.

"To be fearless," she informed them, in a barely shaking voice, "you have to confront your fears."

Confronting fears, Alice decided, was horrible. Her stomach flipped into her mouth, then lurched to her guts before settling to spin uncontrollably somewhere near her lungs. Her palms grew so damp she thought they could never grip the rope. A hundred miles beneath her, the cove was a blurred mess of white and blue.

"Eyes straight ahead," said Jesse, somewhere on a different planet. "One hand over the other. You can do it."

Step by excruciating step, she inched toward the cove. Jesse, lying on the grass with his face and shoulders hanging over the edge of the cliff, grew smaller, his encouragements fainter. The crash of the waves grew louder. Her blood began to dance, her fingers and toes to tingle. This was easy. It was almost fun. All she had to do, to reach the bottom, was . . .

"There's a boat!" Fergus's shout broke into her concentration. She glanced up, saw that he had climbed to the top of the highest battlement, Jesse's binoculars clamped to his eyes.

Alice's world grew fuzzy again.

"Alice!" Barney's shout floated up from miles below, urgent. "You have to hurry!"

"Don't push her!" Jesse yelled. "She's scared of heights!"

Surely, Alice thought with sudden clarity, Barney knew that?

Something was shifting again in Alice's mind. The vertigo, which she had always thought started when Mum died—it hadn't started immediately, but weeks after the funeral, when Alice had climbed up her favorite tree because Dad had gone away, and refused to come down until he came back, and then panicked, and froze . . . In the end, Aunt Patience had had to call the fire brigade. Everyone knew that story.

She saw it now. It wasn't Mum's death that had made her fearful, it was Barney. Barney, who could charm a furious boy with a well-told story . . . Barney with his snow angels and escapades . . .

Barney, who could always make her do exactly what he wanted . . . whom she was always looking for in her dreams, running down empty hallways . . .

"It's not the Leopard!" Fergus yelled. "The boat! It's the coast guard! The coast guard! They're . . . NO! They're heading to the landing jetty! They haven't seen us! Over here! Over here! Come back!"

"Alice!" Barney was panicking now. "Alice, please!"

Slowly but steadily, she resumed her descent. One hand over the other, step by step, but when she reached the bottom of the cliff, she held on to the rope.

"Alice, hurry!" He was waving her over, already pushing the

boat toward the sea. Alice didn't move. She wondered if he would even wait for the others.

"Where will you go?" she shouted.

"What?"

"When you have the money? Where will you go?"

He was walking over, still half turned toward the boat. "Can we talk about this later?"

"No," she said. "I want to talk about it now."

He ran his hands through his hair, so that it stuck up all over his head. Alice used to love it when he did that. Sometimes, he did it on purpose to make her laugh, crossing his eyes and pulling his shirt sideways until he was a disheveled mess, and Alice a writhing, giggling heap, until Patience would invariably say, "For heaven's sake, Barney, grow up!"

But that was the thing, she realized. He was supposed to be the grown-up. He was the one who should be telling them what to do — not a twelve-year-old boy like Jesse with a twisted ankle, still hanging anxiously over the cliff. And it wasn't Alice's fault that they were here — not entirely. It was his. She saw that now.

Even so — one last time, because she loved him, she gave him the benefit of the doubt. It wasn't as if anyone had actually been hurt, he had said . . . And if the money was for them . . . If he would only say that he had done it so that they would never again be separated, that he would never disappear again on trips that they all knew had nothing to do with the theater—if he would only say that he loved her, Alice thought, with a sudden stab of pain.

The way Aunt Patience did, she realized, in every single one of her letters. The way Fergus had told her at Calva—do you remember?—and even Jesse had begrudgingly admitted.

"What will you do with the money?" she repeated.

"I . . . I don't know," Barney faltered. "I haven't really thought."

Alice turned away.

"There's another boat!" Fergus yelled from the top of the cliff. "I think it's the Leopard! It is the Leopard!"

Alice took the rope in both hands.

"Is everything OK?" Jesse called down.

"Alice, what are you doing?" Barney had run up to her now, and was pleading. "Alice, come to the boat!"

"No thank you," she said very politely. "I think I'd rather take my chances with the cliff."

Afterwards, she said it felt as if the world had slowed right down. She looked up and saw her friends, Fergus's skinny silhouette outlined against the sky on the battlement, Jesse's anxious face pinched with pain, and she thought about how much they had done for her. Then she looked at Barney and knew that he would never change.

"I love you, Dad." She sniffed, wiped her nose on her sleeve, rubbed away her tears with the heels of her hands, then pulled him close for a brief, fierce hug. "And I'll miss you, but I'm used to that. And now you'd better go."

One hand over the other, eyes in front, legs braced as Jesse had told her, she started to climb. Unafraid, up and up, never looking down and never stopping, not even when she heard the sound of an engine starting below, or when the sky exploded with purple smoke.

Fearless.

Her mother would have been proud.

FORTY-TWO

Sunday

THE FIREWORK FERGUS had picked up by the loch, tightly sealed in its plastic bag in his rucksack, was miraculously still dry, as was the lighter. "Why did you even bring that?" Jesse shouted as it went up.

"Like those flares sailors use at sea if they're in trouble," Fergus called down from the battlement. "I just thought it might be useful. Don't tell me how many rules I'm breaking, Jesse. Call me a genius instead!"

"Did they see the flare?" cried Alice, rolling off the top of the rope onto the cliff. "Is the coast guard coming?"

"I can't see, the boat's gone behind a headland . . . Jesse, are you watching the Leopard?"

"They're still heading this way—Alice, pull up the rope so they can't climb up if they land! It'll buy us some time, at least, until the coast guard gets here . . . No, wait! I think they've . . .

The Leopard's turning! She's going after Mr. Mistlethwaite . . .
Fergus, what's happening?"

"I still can't see the coast guard . . ."

They sat and looked out to sea—Fergus from his perch,
Alice and Jesse from the cliff—and tried to reassure each other.

"Dad . . ." said Alice. "The Leopard . . ."

"She won't catch him," Jesse said as the boats sped away. "He's
got a head start, and a way bigger boat. I'm more worried about
us. What if they don't find us?"

"We'll go back to the jetty when the tide goes out."

"But the boat's gone! And we don't have any food! Or a tent.
And I can't walk."

"We'll fish!" shouted Fergus from the battlement. "We'll find
a cave! We'll carry you if we have to!"

"And there'll always be another boat tomorrow," said Alice.

They fell silent, eyes still riveted on the waves.

"Hey." Jesse nudged her. "You OK?"

"I will be." She leaned her head, very briefly, on his shoulder.
"Fergus is right—parents are useless."

"Some parents," said Jesse fairly.

Alice looked away, pretending there was something in her
eye, and Jesse offered no help but pretended to believe her. Her
tears wiped away, she pointed at his foot with a shaky smile.

"You've got to stop looking back when you run, Jesse."

He grinned. "One day I'll learn."

Alice watched and watched as the boats bearing Barney and the Leopard grew smaller and smaller, until they were nothing more than dots on the horizon.

"Anything?" Jesse yelled up at Fergus.

"Nothing!"

"Now?" Jesse asked a minute later.

"Still noth— Wait! Yes! Yes! Yes!" Fergus was on his feet, jumping up and down, waving like a lunatic. "They're coming this way! They saw my flare! I'm a genius! Look at me! Look at me! Guys, wave! We're here! Oh my God, the major's with them! And Madoc!"

And they heard the boom of the coast guard's horn.

Alice and Fergus let the rope back out, but the three runaways didn't go down to the beach. Now that they were about to be rescued, they didn't want it to be over.

They all lay on the grass at the top of the cliff, waiting for the boat to arrive, as gulls and shags and puffins and guillemots went about their busy lives around them. They looked up at the cloudless sky, and the boys talked while Alice thought.

"I've made a decision," said Jesse. "I'm going to give up the violin. You absolutely do not need the violin to be an explorer."

"Good for you," said Fergus. "I'm going to stop pulling stupid pranks and focus on being brilliant at something. Like crime. Or maybe ornithology. I haven't decided which yet. Maybe I'll do both."

Jesse grunted approval.

"What about you, Alice?" Fergus asked. "What are you going to do?"

Alice answered with a question. "Would you mind," she said, "when they ask why we did it, if we didn't tell them the truth?"

"To protect your dad?" Fergus, whose appreciation of Barney had not improved, looked mutinous.

"That," Alice said. "But also—I've still got the carving."

FORTY-THREE

A Million Euros

THERE WERE CONSEQUENCES. The major, having rescued them from the island with Madoc and the coast guard, subjected them to a barrage of interrogation, which stopped briefly when Madoc pointed out that they were hurt and started again after first aid had been applied.

Fergus, to his great satisfaction, got his dramatic rescue. Back on Lumm, a doctor was consulted. The police were called and informed that the children had been found. An email was sent out to all parents from a hotel, claiming (falsely) that at no point had the children been in danger, and a press release was issued to satisfy the disaster-hungry local media.

The children's families descended on Stormy Loch — Aunt Patience, Jesse's mother and two of his brothers, and both of Fergus's parents. There were tears and recriminations but also tight, fierce hugs, so that none of the three could doubt how very much they were loved.

Through it all, they made no mention of carvings, Italians, or fathers, and stoutly professed a previously unspoken passion for seabirds.

"Particularly puffins," said Fergus. "They're amazing."

To which the major replied, "The devil with puffins! In Iceland, they boil puffins for breakfast!" and stated that he wanted a Full Report on the Ornithological Significance of the Isle of Nish, together with Geological, Botanical, and Scientific Points of Interest, as well as a Complete History of the People of the West Coast of Scotland from the Vikings to the Present Day, to be presented to the whole school with the aid of photographs, videos, and preferably a couple of songs at the next morning assembly.

"AND WHEN YOU'VE FINISHED, YOU CAN CLEAN THE MINIBUS!" he roared. "WHILE I DECIDE WHETHER OR NOT TO EXPEL THE LOT OF YOU!"

After which he locked himself in his study and began to obsessively check his inbox for emails from parents saying they were removing their children from school. There were no such emails, but he kept checking anyway. After the Unfortunate Incident involving the van Boek girl and the chemistry lab only last term, Stormy Loch did not need bad publicity.

They literally could not afford it.

He fell asleep on the sofa, covered in kittens, and he was still there when Alice knocked on his door the following morning.

"I came to say it was all my fault." She stood in the middle of the room, facing the open window because she couldn't quite meet the major's eyes. "It was my idea to go to the island. I was . . . looking for something, I suppose. Someone told me about it. They made it sound wonderful—like a story in a book. I'm sorry—I can't really explain. But I just wanted to make it clear, about the boys. I'm the one who should be punished."

The major, addled from sleep and with an adolescent cat kneading his leg with its paws, stared at the small girl standing very straight before him and wondered what on earth he was supposed to say, let alone do.

"When you do punish me," Alice faltered, "it would be very nice if you didn't expel me."

The major found that something was tickling his nose. Also, slightly prickling his eyes. He cleared his throat very loudly.

"The island, was it wonderful?" he asked. "Did you find what you were looking for?"

Alice stared very hard out the window.

"I didn't find what I was looking for, no. But I do think I may have found what I wanted."

The major followed her gaze outside.

It was Sunday, and Stormy Loch was at play. The rowboats were out in force on emerald-green water. Someone was playing a guitar near the music tower, and a rowdy football game was taking place on the sports field. These were sights and sounds to lift his heart, but not, he suspected, what Alice was gazing at so fiercely. He looked closer, searching for details—ah, there they were! Jesse Okuyo, sitting with his mother and brothers on a bench facing the loch, and Fergus Mackenzie walking along the shore, holding hands with both his parents, and Alice's aunt on the jetty with . . . Madoc?

"She's a really good artist," said Alice. "And you need a new art teacher."

"I do," admitted the major.

"She loves it here," said Alice. "We both do."

"You do?" The major felt quite extraordinarily pleased. "So do I!"

"Then we can stay?"

He tried to be stern. "Have you actually spoken to your aunt about this?"

"Not yet." Alice beamed. "But I'm sure I can convince her."

"I've no doubt you can," he said dryly. "And yes—you can stay."

Alice's smile lit up the room.

"Thank you! Thank you so much! You can punish me any

other way you want! I promise I won't complain a bit. From now on, I'll be a model of excellent behavior!"

"I'll look forward to that."

She skipped toward the door, then stopped and walked back toward him, fumbling for something in her jacket pocket.

"I nearly forgot," she said (unconvincingly, the major thought afterwards). "We found this too."

She dropped something into his hand, smooth and surprisingly warm, about the size of a plum.

"It was just lying on the beach," she said, and was gone before he could react.

He knew exactly what it was but checked online just to be sure. There it was, the whole story—the little jade figure, the impossible robbery, the colossal reward . . .

And it was just lying on the beach?

It wasn't possible—was it? He should ask questions. There was a story here, and it was his duty as a responsible headmaster to get to the bottom of it.

On the other hand . . .

A million euros, the major thought. *What the school could do with a million euros . . .*

He watched from his tower as Alice ran out to the jetty to hug her aunt, danced back to Jesse's bench, waved at Fergus. A different child from the one who had arrived at the beginning of term, so lost and so troublesome. A happy child. He had been right to take her in, despite the lack of school fees.

A million euros . . . He couldn't. Could he?

But what was he supposed to do? He couldn't very well keep the jade carving! And if someone was offering good money for it . . .

His eye fell on the door of his office, repainted just last week a particularly violent shade of mauve. The guitar's song outside reminded him that the recent renovation of the music tower was still not paid for. And just before leaving for Lumm, he had received a telephone call from another headmistress about a child —a good child, but a troubled one who had just been expelled and, like so many waifs and strays, could do well with a new beginning.

A million euros . . .

The major placed the boy and dragon carefully on his desk and picked up the phone.

And Then . . .

THINK OF A ROSEBUSH, by a loch. The bush is positively exploding with flowers, blowsy white roses that ramble up and over a stone wall, reaching into trees, twining through and over shrubs. It is the most beautiful, most riotous rosebush you have ever seen in your life. When the wind blows—and it very often does blow here at Stormy Loch—it looks like the roses are dancing.

The rosebush isn't actually here yet, but it will be. Alice has emailed Patience and told her she has to bring it next term, when she comes to be the new art teacher. She has looked up online how to transplant a rosebush. Together, she and Patience will find a sheltered, south-facing wall and dig a big hole, into which they will pour water and rake manure from the farm. Then, very carefully so as not to damage the roots, they will plant Clara Kaminska Mistlethwaite's rosebush, and over the next few years they will watch it grow even stronger and more joyful than it was at Cherry Grange.

Just like Alice herself.

Meanwhile . . . Ah, meanwhile . . .

Picture a lot of kids in boats on the loch. Not just Alice and Fergus and Jesse, but Samira, Jenny, and Duffy too, Amir and Esme and Zuzu and Zeb. On land, some art students were enthusiastically hurling splodges of multicolored paint over Frau Kirschner's Exploding Butterfly. It's late — it's so late! It's past ten o'clock in the evening, and tomorrow is a school day, and all of these young people ought to be in bed. But the summer term is becoming exactly what the major said it would, with days that go on forever and nights that feel like day. The sun disappeared ages ago behind the mountains and still the sky is light, with a smattering of pale stars and a sliver of moon, and the twilight seems to glow.

Nobody ever wants to go to bed!

Last night, this same band of kids sneaked out of school for a not-very-secret midnight picnic up the valley. Tonight, they're meant to be fishing.

As a fishing party, I have to tell you, they are not successful. To catch fish, it's important to be quiet, and it's best if you're alone, or with just one other person, and you shouldn't talk, let alone shout or laugh. You certainly shouldn't rock boats, or accidentally fall in the water, or when you have accidentally fallen in, try to pull other people after you.

They haven't caught so much as a minnow, but they really don't care.

Just look at them—Jesse and Fergus and Alice! What a long way they've come since we first met. Look at Jesse, our good boy, Captain Fussypants, rocking the boat with his full weight to try and tip Zeb into the water. Look at Fergus, our evil prankster, having a shy, quiet conversation with Samira in a boat a little apart from all the others . . . And look at Alice. Timid, silent Alice, laughing almost as loud as Jenny!

It seems they've all discovered a talent for making friends.

By the time Alice and Fergus and Jesse had returned to school with the major and Madoc, wild rumors about what they had been up to were flying around. And even though they had sworn one another to secrecy, they couldn't avoid the onslaught of questions.

"So!" Jenny dumped her dinner tray down next to Alice's on their first night back. "Is it true your tent was struck by lightning? And Fergus almost died, and Jesse nearly broke his neck?"

"Did you really have to be rescued by helicopter?" asked Duffy. "Did it really have to winch you out of the sea?"

"Yes," Fergus declared. "Absolutely. All of this is true."

"Don't believe him," Jesse mumbled. "It wasn't nearly that dramatic."

"Says the boy who broke into a house!" cried Fergus.

"You broke into a house?" Zeb gawped at Jesse with new respect.

"And I did nearly die," Fergus insisted, and launched into a gruesome, detailed description of his food-poisoning symptoms that made some people turn green and others roar with laughter.

As more and more students crowded round to listen, gasping and laughing and saying, "That bit can't be true!" Alice watched and smiled but did not speak.

Until . . .

"But why?" asked Samira. "Why did you leave the Challenge, when you wanted to win so badly, and go off to an island?"

Fergus and Jesse turned to Alice.

"Wh-what?" she stammered.

"You tell them," said Fergus.

"Me?" Alice stared round the table at a sea of expectant faces. "I can't," she whispered. "You know I can't. You're the one who's good at talking."

"But I don't know what I'm supposed to say," he whispered back. "We agreed—you know—that we wouldn't mention . . ."

"I can't do it!"

"Alice, he's *your* dad!"

And so Alice, for the first time in her life, told a story to a crowd.

She didn't tell the whole truth, like about Barney being an international criminal and people chasing them with guns. But the story she did tell them, about a crazy marvelous father and the tales he told his daughter, wasn't entirely untrue.

And the way Alice told it . . . ah, the way Alice told it!

It didn't start well.

"The thing is . . ." Her mouth dried up, and she stopped.

Jesse gave her some water. She gulped it gratefully, then coughed as it went down the wrong way. Fergus thumped her on the back.

"The thing is . . ."

Her stomach lurched. It was like vertigo — it was worse than vertigo!

She closed her eyes.

An image came into her mind, of a cliff, and a rope, and a girl climbing away from a beach, up and up toward a bright blue sky, never looking down.

She opened her eyes again.

"Don't tell if you'd rather not," said Samira.

"It's all right," said Alice.

She took a deep breath.

"Imagine an island full of birds, and a rock in the shape of a castle . . ."

The others listened, spellbound, as Alice talked, and talked, and talked.